The Corpse in the Closet

Lake Wilson Mysteries 1

Nancy Monroe

Dedication

For Mom, who taught me two things. One, I could do anything I put my mind to and two, anything could be a murder weapon. Both useful lessons in their own way.

Chapter One
Friday

I was sitting at the bar wondering if I would really get the first bad review of my career because I couldn't find bright orange toilet paper when the elixir of life, aka Diet Coke, was placed in front of me.

"You looked like you needed a refill," Rodney said. Rodney Staltz, Rod to his friends, had been the main bartender at The Dive for the last year. He reminded me of a young Pierce Brosnan. *Remington Steele* young. But without the dashing part of the dashing good looks. And not so much good as okay. All right, maybe he was more Pierce's very distant cousin. But he was tall and had dark hair so that had to count for something. Rodney was a Lake Wilson transplant. His mom moved him and his twin brother here when they were in high school. For Lake Wilson that made him a virtual newbie. Never mind that it had been fifteen years ago.

"Thanks, I do," I said.

"Stressful day?"

"It's the big event tomorrow. The wedding of the year and although the bride and groom are nice enough, the mother of the bride is a little … demanding." I probably shouldn't be talking about Lucy Barton that way, but Rodney had been hired as the DJ and knew how big a deal the whole thing was. Besides, he wasn't one for gossip. I don't think he could say a bad word about someone. *Unlike me.* And he was a bartender, you were supposed to spill your guts to them. It was some kind of unwritten rule.

"You'll be fine, Maddy. Your aura is bright, and your intentions are pure. And, if you need a break, you can come sit next to the DJ. I hear he's the best," he said with a wink. Rodney was a little new-agey for me, but he was trying to make me feel better, so I let it go. "Besides, Sunday morning yoga will get you centered again. Don't forget it's in the park since the weather is getting nicer."

Rodney and I were both in my cousin Cathy's yoga class. He was a much better student then I was, but he was right, I always felt better after. You wouldn't know it by looking or even talking to him, but Rodney had picked up yoga while he was in prison of all places. He never really talked about how he ended up there, just that it allowed him to find his purpose in life. His goal was to save up enough money to move to Tibet—or was it Nepal?—and study with monks there. Or something. Once he got to words I couldn't pronounce I tended to nod and zone out.

"Thanks, Rodney. Lucy Barton is a force to be reckoned with in Lake Wilson. If we have a social hierarchy, she is perched firmly at the top. Her daughter, Stacy, is perfectly reasonable. And all the groom, Carl, cares about is marrying Stacy. They are a cute couple. It should be about them, but Lucy can't stand not being the center of attention."

"Hey, Maddy. Hey, Rod." I turned to see Tommy Stempler, one of my two best friends since kindergarten (which was longer ago then I wanted to admit) walk in from the kitchen. I shouldn't have been surprised, since he owned The Dive, but I didn't realize he was working today.

"Hey, Tommy," Rodney and I greeted in unison and then smiled at each other.

"How's it going?" he asked.

"Lucy Barton," was all I had to say.

"Got it." He sat down next to me and ordered potato skins. Since he was mostly a healthy eater, I knew they were for me. Gotta love a best friend who respects your addiction to plastic cheese.

At six feet and built like a MAC truck, Tommy had been a linebacker in high school and still looked like he could play. When he shaved his head, we called him Mr. Clean for a while and tried to get him to pierce an ear to complete the look. Yeah, that was a no go. You could pretty much always find him wearing jeans and a Dive shirt, working behind the bar. If he wasn't here, he was at the gym since one of the few things he was religious about was working out. Every morning at 6 a.m., you would find him there. Sometimes you even found his fiancée, Mateo, with him, although not often. They had been together since college and had finally decided to marry. Jess, our partner in crime, and I were biting at the bit to begin planning as soon as they said we could start. We had a whole list of ideas.

Tommy was the epitome of a hometown boy. He was born and raised here, went to community college so he could commute from home. In addition to owning The Dive, he had recently started buying commercial property and investing back in the town. He truly loved this town, even more so when everyone was so accepting of him coming out in college. I don't think you could get him out of Lake Wilson with dynamite.

Luckily, Mateo loved this place just as much. Where Tommy was a lifer, Mateo was new to town when they met in college. And where Tommy was quiet and reserved, Mateo was the life of the party. He could be a double for Fabio except he never broke five feet, nine inches. It was impossible not to love Mateo. He just oozed happiness and joy. I don't think I ever saw him anything but smiling. He endeared himself to everyone he met and we all loved him for loving Tommy.

I was just about to lament to Tommy on the trials and tribulations of custom dyed toilet paper when the door slammed open and in walked the third member of our posse. *Is three really a posse?*

"Rodney Staltz, where the hell have you been all morning?" Jessica March yelled from the other side of the room. Apparently, we were getting Hurricane Jess today. I thought back to the schedule and suddenly realized why she was upset. While I was stressing about toilet paper, she was directing the run through of the vendors for the wedding. Where I was merely acting as her assistant brought in to help, she was the Event Coordinator for the Lake Wilson Resort and Spa, known in town as "The Resort." I was suddenly very glad I was not Rodney.

"I left a message. One of the cats at the pet sanctuary was being put down this morning because she had cancer. I had to comfort the other animals. I knew they would be able to tell there was something going on. You know animals are very sensitive to changes in energy. They needed extra attention," he tried explaining.

"You know what else needs special attention, Rodney? The wedding you are DJing for tomorrow. Do you know how hard it is to run through an event when the music isn't there to run through the cues and timing? Do you?"

3

Jess was on a roll now.

"I'm sorry, Jess. No matter what I will be there tomorrow. I promise," he tried assuring her.

"You had better be. Do you need me to text you to make sure you are awake and on your way in the morning?" she asked.

"I don't have a cell phone. They are bad for your blood pressure. And unplugging is necessary for a peaceful life." He closed his eyes and took a deep breath.

"You know what else is necessary for a peaceful life? Not missing tomorrow's wedding." Jess also took a deep breath and her shoulders visibly relaxed.

Just then, one of the cooks brought out my potato skins and placed them in front of me. I closed my laptop as Jess came over and sat on the other side of me, picking up a skin. *It's a Maddy sandwich.* I knew she was upset when she reduced herself to eating something as tame as a potato skin. Suicide wings were more her speed.

Jess was just over five feet, six inches and stunningly beautiful. Her mom had been a successful model in the late seventies (one of the first African American models to make a successful career in what was an all-white industry then) and her father was a college English professor. Jess inherited her mother's good looks and her father's ability to command a room. She had light coffee skin, a result of being biracial, and light brown eyes that reflected every emotion. Her mom "retired" to move to Lake Wilson and opened the local party supply and stationary store after meeting and falling in love with Mr. Murphy. You would have thought it would have been a step down from modeling, but she seemed to love it and the Murphys were the kind of couple everyone wanted to be ... still in love after all these years. Now the store was run by Jess's nephews and Mrs. Murphy was usually found there socializing with customers.

I, on the other hand, was the taller, curvier kid with light brown curly hair and blue eyes. I inherited my father's height and my mother's smart mouth. Everyone said I was the perfect fifty-fifty mix of both of them, and it's probably true. My mom's family was the "unconventional" type. They had moved to Lake Wilson when Mom was just a kid after leaving some kind of post WWII commune to settle down. Dad's family had been here since it was founded and was as strait-laced as you could get. But opposites attract and it was love at first sight. I was an only child, which made my parents the oddity in both their families. They had recently retired and were traveling the country in an RV, enjoying all the nooks and crannies the world had to offer.

In Lake Wilson, a disproportionate segment of the population was related to me. I was the product of two families that had lots of kids and those kids had lots of kids. At least by modern standards. My dad was one of six and my mom was one of four and all of their siblings had multiple children. The fact I was the only "only child" of the whole bunch only served to make me stand out even more.

I'm not sure if it was being an only child or something else, but Tommy, Jess, and I were as close as you could be. She and Tommy were godparents to my daughter Megan and son MJ (Mitch Junior). Her fifteen-year-old twins were my godchildren. After years of struggling to get pregnant and fertility treatments, Jess and her husband Rob had given up hoping and were considering adoption when they found out they were expecting. It was the most nerve racking eight months of my life after she got the positive test. I wasn't that nervous during my own pregnancies.

While Jess had an older brother and a sister, Tommy and I had adopted her as our sister. We had created our own "family" of sorts and our kids were more like cousins. They say you can't pick your relatives, but you can pick your friends. We decided somewhere on the playground in third grade that the sentiment was a stupid adult rule and decided we would be a family. It had worked for us ever since.

Now I often got the chance to work with Jess because we had similar roles in different spheres. Jess had started working at The Resort in the events department during college and had been there ever since. The Resort was originally a sprawling sixty room mansion built by the Benton-Endicotts at the end of the nineteenth century. Charles Benton-Endicott Jr. was a Philadelphia financier who built the mansion for his family to enjoy during their yearly ten-week summer vacations to Lake Wilson. Why a family of four needed sixty rooms no one knew, but they did. And it was truly magnificent. It always reminded me somewhat of The Breakers in Newport, Rhode Island. The home was originally named Magnolia Farms but as the home was neither a farm nor grew magnolias the name never really caught on. In the 1960s, the Zuckman family bought it at auction when the Benton-Endicotts had managed to blow through their once considerable fortune. The Zuckman's had added to The Resort over the years and it now had 500 guest rooms, a golf course, tennis courts, a spa, and plenty of facilities for conferences and events such as tomorrow's wedding.

How and why the Benton-Endicotts had chosen Lake Wilson for their sprawling estate was anyone's guess. Prior to their arrival, the lake itself had very few homes around it and the adjoining town was small. At the time, there were less than 500 permanent residents who called the town home and most of them were farmers. Now the town was larger, though not by much, and the lake was a regular retreat for tens of thousands in the summer. The farms had given way to summer cabins and a shopping center. And the population grew by tenfold during the summer months. Thankfully, most of the temporary residents invaded lake homes only and left the town to the yearlong inhabitants. It meant the town kept itself to its original compact design instead of becoming a sprawling suburban mass. Most businesses were along the cross streets of Main and Elm with the residential streets off them. Main took you in and out of town on county roads while Elm took you to the lake roads and Interstate. The town itself was fairly walkable, and no one was eager to see that change. Traffic backed up on the weekends during the warmer months, but it was a small price to pay for the quaintness the permanent residents enjoyed.

"So, do I need to ask how the run through went?" I knew this was a big event for Jess for a few reasons. In addition to being the biggest social event of the year for Lake Wilson and the biggest wedding The Resort had handled in a while, Jess was looking to move up into management of The Resort. She needed this to go off without a hitch so a raving Lucy Barton wouldn't make an appearance.

"Very funny, Maddy. The only saving grace was that Lucy Barton couldn't be there due to family obligations. She would have had a cow otherwise. And I would have been on the receiving end of a major chewing out," she said. "I'm telling you, Tommy, if Rodney messes up tomorrow, I don't know if I'll kill him or you first. You vouched for him."

"I know. He'll be there. He promised, and that means something to Rodney," Tommy replied. "Those animals are his heart and soul, but when he promises he'll be there he shows."

~~~

It wasn't until I was in bed later that night that I started to reflect on where life had brought me. I had left Lake Wilson to go to college vowing to conquer the world. I had come home twenty years later with two teen kids and no career to speak of. I had gotten to see the world courtesy of my ex's career but relocating at the whim of the corporate world was not conducive to me pursuing a career. I decided to exchange *my* dreams for *our* dreams. And it had worked. At least for a while. Until *our* dreams became *his* dreams and by then I had had enough.

Now I was a successful event planner in my hometown and had a fairly rich life. My kids were launched and happy. I was surrounded by a loving family and supportive friends. I got to explore any hobby or interest I had without someone complaining it took up too much time. And I had plenty of Diet Coke in the fridge. All in all, life was going along very well and my biggest concern was if Lucy Barton was going to take issue with the passed hors d'oeuvres tomorrow. *Please, let her like the passed hors d'oeuvres*

Chapter Two

Saturday

There is a reason God invented playlists. Getting your heart rate up during a workout, long soaks in the bathtub to relax after a hard day's work, dancing while cooking dinner. Road trips … road trips are a great reason for playlists. But what's not a great reason for a playlist? To cover for missing DJs at the social event of the year. Nevertheless, I did have a playlist for just such an occasion. Or at least I had one I had been working on as part of my event planner toolkit. I wouldn't have called it a completed work of art, but beggars can't be choosers. And right now, my best friend was begging.

"Please tell me you have something you can put on. The guests are going to be here any minute," Jess implored. She was tapping her two-inch heels that matched perfectly with her light blue silk sheath dress that stopped just above her knees. How she could work an event in heels, I will never know. Especially since she had been here since 8 a.m. making sure everything was perfect. Jess's shoe collection rivaled Imelda Marcos's and I don't think there was a pair of flats in her closet. She was also an avid runner (just proof no one is perfect), so she looked amazing in heels despite the fact she ate anything she wanted. It was one of the few things about her I hated. But seeing as we have been best friends since kindergarten, I let it slide.

After almost forty years of friendship, I knew the foot tapping was the first sign of a prospective meltdown. When recounting the story later, Jess would move from begging to imploring status but right now, I just felt bad for her. This was, after all, one of the, if not *the* biggest social events of the year. It wasn't every day the only daughter of one of the oldest families in Lake Wilson got married. And Jess was in charge of the entire event, so it was her neck on the line.

"Of course, I do. I just have to connect the playlist to the speakers. I'm sure we can make it work," I replied with far more confidence than I possessed. Randomly hitting buttons had always worked for me in the past, why would it fail me now? All else failing, my daughter the computer genius was on speed dial. And she would do just about anything for her Aunt Jess.

"Don't worry, Robby can handle that. Where is it? Please, tell me you put it in a cloud or somewhere equally magical? The laptop is connected to the speakers by some kind of voodoo," Jess explained. The foot tapping had slowed once I started typing. I guess she was buying my fake it till we make it attitude. You would have thought as a resort event coordinator she would have these kinds of speed bumps handled but the bride's mother, Lucy Barton, had been driving us both crazy with last minute "updates." I wasn't regretting charging her a premium now.

I logged into my Spotify account on the laptop Jess pointed at disdainfully and started my four-hour wedding mix. Her disgust for the laptop was somewhat ironic since her husband Robby was a math and computer science teacher at the local high school, but everyone has their demons and technology has always been Jess's. Even in high school, no one could ruin a tape in a Walkman faster than she could. Next thing I knew, "Fly Me To The Moon" by Sinatra was playing through every speaker in the ballroom. I could see Jess's shoulders relax and knew we had averted a crisis. When I took over my late Aunt Aggie's event planning business, I never imagined I would be filling in as DJ at the wedding of the year.

In my six years as the owner of An Affair to Remember, I had found myself in a lot of roles. Where Aunt Aggie had pretty much stuck to charity galas, I had expanded the business to take on any event big or small. What can I say ... I like a good party. After my divorce and the kids going off to college, I needed something to fill my time. In almost twenty years of marriage and even longer parenting, I had thrown more than my share of parties and seemed to have a natural talent for it. And it allowed Aunt Aggie to keep up to date on all the good town events, and therefore gossip, without having to work too hard. It was times like this I missed our after-event talks. She called them

9

"debriefings," but I think that is because she had a thing for spy stories.

My next thought was that Rodney needed to show up to take over his duties before the first dance. I'm sure we could handle introducing the wedding party since we had drafted the program, but when it came to actual music choices, I was clueless. I had no idea what song the newly married Stacy and Carl Franklin had picked for their first dance and I don't think they wanted me picking one on the spot. Gloria Gaynor's "I Will Survive" was probably not fitting. What could I say, I'm slightly jaded when it comes to marriage.

"Where the hell did Rodney go? He was here setting up earlier. I'm never letting him work another event in my resort again," Jess railed. And seeing as she was the Senior Event Coordinator for the Lake Wilson Resort and Spa she could actually follow through with the threat. The Resort was the classiest and most expensive facility in three counties. As such, there was no other venue that would do for the wedding of Lucy and Reginald Barton's only daughter. Lucy and Reggie were considered pillars of society and were not about to let the wedding of their only daughter be anything but *the* social even of the year. "No other venue will do," was her exact quote. Lucy was known for her over the top style and so when her daughter announced her engagement a year ago, Jess got a call the following morning booking the Grand Ballroom for the perfect spring wedding. It was also around that time that Lucy adopted a never before heard Southern accent, but that discussion is for another day.

Stacy's only real request was the color scheme be inspired by her favorite flower, orange gerbera daisies. I have to admit I was a little worried when I first heard that. It's not that Stacy was an inherently tacky person. Honestly, she was just sort of plain. If it had been left to her and Carl, they probably would have eloped to a justice of the peace and then hit up a Harry Potter movie marathon. But Stacy had turned the entire event over to her mother and the two were not cut from the same cloth.

"All I want is to end the day married to Carl," I remember her saying. "Honestly, if Mother weren't so hell bent on a big wedding we would probably be eloping. But I can't let her down." Stacy had been almost sad when she said it but true to her word, she had not created drama and agreed with everything Lucy suggested so long as it would still end with her being Mrs. Carl Franklin.

"There's only one request I have," she had finally said. "I love gerbera daisies and would like the color scheme to reflect that." Jess and I had been thrilled when she finally gave us some hint of what she actually wanted. Luckily, Lucy hadn't given any push back. Lucy's best friend, Kay Morgan, was the florist who had been hired for the wedding and assured her they could do "magnificent things" with gerbera daisies. I'm not sure what qualified as magnificent, but I had to admit, looking around, the flowers added to the atmosphere.

It really was a beautiful wedding. Not my style, but there was no denying that everyone went all out. French doors lined one long side that lead out to a patio overlooking the lake. Tonight, the doors had classic white drapes held back with bright sashes to match the wedding color scheme. The opposite wall had doorways that lead to The Resort where guests entered. We'd left them open since there were no other events today. The cross wind was subtle, but enough to keep the room from getting too warm. One side was set up with an elevated stage for bands or VIP tables. The wedding party was supposed to be sitting there after the ceremony. It actually allowed for them to have a little bit of down time and enjoy themselves separate from the rest of the guests.

The tables and chairs were wrapped in white to create a striking contrast to the colored sashes and bright flowers everywhere. The centerpieces were gorgeous arrangements of daisies and baby's breath and were elevated to allow dinner conversation, which was the new norm lately at The Resort. The only oddity was the choice in elevation aide. The arrangements were sitting in the palm of a foot high crystal cherub, toga diaper and all. I couldn't say I had seen them before, and I had no idea where Kay had found them. Honestly, I thought they were a little creepy. I might even have nightmares of them attacking me like something out of Hitchcock's *The Birds*. But guests were squealing about how cute they were. To each his own.

The Resort also had a reputation to uphold for providing your dream event where any request could be accommodated. Jess often had to get creative with making those dreams come true but so far no one had gone away unhappy. Luckily, today's wedding didn't require jugglers or fire eaters but that didn't guarantee smooth sailing for those working to make Stacy's dreams come true. Although, in all honesty, if a missing emcee was all Jess and I were going to have to deal with then the day would go down as a win.

Sinatra had given way to Josh Groban, the hors d'oeuvres were ready for the guests now arriving from the ceremony, and there was no sign of my ex-husband, yet. We got along well enough at events for our kids, but outside of that, I had no urge to talk to him. It was a win all around.

All that was missing was Rodney.

Chapter Three

Rule number one of event planning is own comfortable shoes. It was three hours into the reception before I finally got a chance to sit down and take a breather and I was congratulating myself on wearing something rather comfortable. I had decided on a pair of black slacks and a pink embroidered silk kimono combo for the wedding. These were my favorite pants because they were long enough to hide my comfy flats and still looked formal. Thankfully Carl's brother took over music duties and wasn't half bad. With that, I finally had a chance to sit back and appreciate another successful event.

Even though everything was going smoothly, this was my first chance to sit since it was just part of my nature to double check and make sure nobody needed help. By the time I was confident that the world would continue to revolve if I took a ten-minute break, I was starved. I consider it part of my job in quality control to hit up the buffet and make sure I had a sampling of as much as possible. Jess had hired a new caterer, Jean-Paul, for the wedding so really it was market research. He had recently settled in Lake Wilson and had been getting rave reviews from all the developers that had been working on the Lake Wilson project that was expanding the number of vacation homes in our area. *Yippee!* That's how I found myself in one of the corner tables finally getting a chance to indulge in a bit of everything that was offered.

As I got settled, I caught myself looking around at all the tables to make sure there were no issues and found myself distracted by the cherub centerpieces. A chill ran up my back.

"I think they are going to replace clowns in my nightmares," Jess confessed as she sat next to me with an overflowing plate of her own. She really could read my mind sometimes.

"I have to think they were Lucy's idea. I cannot see Stacy being a fan of cherubs," I said. One of the few things I knew about Stacy was she was a huge fantasy and horror fan. That was how she and Carl had actually met. They happened to strike up a conversation while in line at a book signing of their favorite author and the rest was history. What is surprising is that Lake Wilson is a small town but somehow they had managed not to run into each other before that day. Whereas Stacy was born and bred here, Carl only moved here two years ago when he got a job at the local police department. Considering they were both introverts, they were lucky to stumble onto each other at all. They honestly made one of the cutest couples I had worked with in a while, and I was really hoping they got their happily ever after.

"Speaking of Lucy, I think she is headed in our direction," Jess warned.

I looked up in time to see both Lucy and Kay heading our way. I put on my best professional smile and got ready to find out how we had done.

"Ladies, isn't it the most beautiful wedding," Kay greeted. I took a deep breath and realized that Kay would be an ally. I forgot that although she may be Lucy's friend, she was still working the wedding as much as Jess and I were.

"Thank you all for your hard work. I don't think I could have done it without you," Lucy gushed. She literally sounded like an Oscar acceptance speech.

"We were just glad we could help you all have such a memorable day," Jess said. She was so good at this kind of thing. It's one of the reasons she was so successful.

"It really did turn out beautifully. Everyone seems to have had a lovely time," I said, observing the guests who were laughing, dancing, and enjoying themselves. I wasn't sure with the guest list variety how the reception would work out. Stacy's side was mostly the equivalent of Lake Wilson high society while Carl's was his fellow police officers and the working class of Lake Wilson. I think the Chief of Police approved just about everyone's leave to attend. If you were going to rob a bank in Lake Wilson, today would be the perfect day to do it.

"Thank you all for your hard work. It's too bad we didn't have time to see about the bathroom accessories being color coordinated, but everything really came together," Lucy finished. She and Kay turned around and dismissed us. Or rather excused themselves.

"Bathroom accessories?" Jess asked me.

"She originally wanted me to change the soap dispensers and flowers in The Resort bathrooms to match the wedding colors. She also asked if I could find custom dyed toilet paper," I replied. Jess rolled her eyes. "I knew changing something like that was not going to happen so I just told Lucy that we wouldn't be able to get the properly dyed items in time since it was one of those last-minute things she brought up." *That has to be on the internet somewhere doesn't it?*

"Well, the staff will be thrilled when this is over and she's not correcting everything and 'fixing' the place settings. You would think we had never done a wedding before," Jess complained. I made a mental note to add to the staff tip for having to deal with Lucy.

After checking my watch, I knew the limo had arrived to take Stacy and Carl away for the night and The Resort staff would soon handle clean up, so as far as I was concerned most of my work was done. All that was left was to make sure everything, tuxes and other rental items, were returned on Monday.

"Plans for tomorrow?" I asked before taking a bite of beef wellington. I think I may have actually moaned out loud. Jean-Paul had really knocked it out of the park. I mean, who picks beef wellington for a buffet and still manages to make it amazing? I was going to have to get his contact information from Jess. A solid caterer was worth their weight in gold.

"Sleeping in and then forcing the kids to help with yard work. I want to get my flowers planted before the wedding season really ramps up. Once that happens, I'll never be home on the weekends. I have flats of peonies for the twins to plant in the front and Rob has plans for the back so I am going to put my feet up and delegate. What about you?" she asked.

"I have yoga then plan on stopping by A Slice of Heaven for something decadent. Probably spend all day reading and not worrying about if we have all the tuxes for return. It's my decompress day," I replied, dreaming of my reading chair and cheesecake. Rodney was in my yoga class so when he showed up tomorrow, I was going to have a serious talk to him about blowing off a job this big. In all honesty, I was surprised he'd dropped the ball. He didn't strike me as being flaky. But it just goes to show you don't know people as well as you think you do.

"So, I think it's safe to say we can eliminate gerbera daisies as a theme for Tommy and Mateo," I said. Ever since Tommy got engaged Jess and I had been putting together ideas for when they finally set a date. Every wedding one of us handled came under strict scrutiny to see if there were ideas we could steal from it.

"Yeah, no. I can't see either of them wanting orange as a main color. Although, I'm tempted to get foot high cherubs for the centerpieces just to see Tommy's reaction." We looked at each other and burst out laughing. There was no way that would fly with him.

"Although, if we said it was Mateo's idea, we might be able to talk him into it," I replied.

"And throw away four decades of friendship when he finds out we lied? No, thank you. I still need his help with the twins. They'll do anything if Uncle Tommy asks."

"Hey, how come that doesn't work for Aunt Maddy?"

Jess shrugged. There was something about Tommy kids flocked to. He was the Pied Piper for all four of our kids.

We fell into a comfortable silence born of friendship and hunger as I sat there thinking how great it had all turned out.

I should have known things were going too well.

Chapter Four

"Bogey at 2 o'clock," Jess suddenly warned. I knew she could only mean my ex-husband Mitch and his wife Heather. Mitch and I have been divorced six years and separated longer, but since he now lived one town over, we still saw more of each other then I would have liked. The divorce wasn't acrimonious so we could at least be pleasant to each other. The kids were in high school and college when we split and now had lives of their own. We didn't even argue about dividing up the assets or alimony. I think we were just both relieved.

When we had gotten married, I had just graduated from college and Mitch had just gotten his MBA. He had landed a great job with a large bank. What he failed to mention until after we got married was that he told them he would be willing to relocate. At first, I was fine with that. I had gotten pregnant right after the wedding and he said that since we would be moving, I should stay home with Megan. What I didn't realize was that he would regularly agree to transfers in pursuit of his moving up in the company. We ended up in San Francisco, Chicago, London, Tokyo, Dallas, and Zurich before I decided I had had enough. But it wasn't the moving around. Even after the adventure of that wore off it still wasn't enough to end a marriage. It was the micromanaging by Mitch.

Every time he was promoted, it was like I was, too. And I needed to look and act the part. I joined the requisite clubs and committees regardless of my personal interests. When he suggested we get a chef so that it would be easier for me to lose weight I hit the ceiling. I'm not going to be confused with a super model anytime soon, but I worked hard to stay healthy. I always struggled with the last fifteen pounds to get to pre-kid shape, but when he suggested I lose forty, I knew it would be like that for the rest of our lives. No matter what I did, he was always going to find something I needed to work on. I realized that somewhere along the line we had gone from being a marriage to being a partnership, a business. And sadly, neither of us noticed until it was too late.

One of the few things I admired about Mitch was his desire to be geographically close to the kids after the divorce. He transferred to an office near us so he could see them on a regular basis. No matter what my complaints were about him as a husband, my kids were very lucky to have him as a father. That didn't mean I wanted to hang out with him at a wedding however. We were, after all, divorced for a reason.

I looked up with a fake smile already plastered on my face. I guess it was too much to ask that I escape the day without seeing him. Heather was part of Lucy's social circle and I knew from the RSVP list they would be attending. But in a reception of three hundred and fifty people I just hoped they would be occupied with socializing and not have time for little ole me. A girl could dream. *Note to self: eat in kitchen with staff from now on.*

"What a lovely wedding, isn't it?" Heather started. Heather isn't so bad, she is just totally different from me. Standing at just five feet, five inches, she is the definition of small boned and dainty. Her always perfectly styled hair could put any model to shame. And I don't think I have ever seen her in anything less than full makeup. Honestly, if she is what Mitch wanted in a wife it is amazing we lasted as long as we did. But she is good to my kids which pretty much means she is fine with me.

She and Mitch met when he was guest speaking at a local college. The story goes she came up after the lecture and asked him for career advice. Since her major had been elementary education, I wasn't sure what she was looking for from an investment consultant. Although, maybe I did know and just liked to give her the benefit of the doubt since she was going to be a part of my life, no matter how indirectly, for a long time. I don't know the exact details since Mitch's post-marriage love life was not something I wanted details on. The only rumors that annoyed me were that it wasn't so much post-marriage as during. But again, I didn't ask because it didn't matter. My indifference was proof enough for me that divorce was the right decision.

17

"It really is. Are you enjoying yourself?" Jess kept it professional. Always looking for feedback on how to make The Resort better, she was genuinely interested in their opinion. And given that Heather and Mitch spent so much time and money at The Resort, she was a "valued customer." They played golf and tennis weekly and ate at one of the on-site restaurants just as often.

"We really are. Weddings are just such a joyous occasion and Stacy and Carl make such a lovely couple." I could tell Heather was about to dive into an in-depth review of every aspect of the wedding when one of Mitch's golfing buddies came over and asked her to dance. Mitch let her float off thankful he didn't have to do the honors. The look of relief on his face was almost comical; he had two left feet on a good day. He turned to me and I could tell he wasn't going to excuse himself.

"To what do I owe the honor?" I asked, knowing he was not hanging around for the scenery. I didn't mean to sound bitchy but I knew what was coming and I would just as soon not revisit the issue. But today my luck had run out.

"I just wanted to see if you thought about my offer further," he asked innocently. My Aunt Agatha was actually his great-aunt and left me her home when she passed. I had adored Aggie and we were great friends and business partners. She fostered my love for solving puzzles and riddles and we spent hours talking about life and working on jigsaw puzzles, crosswords or any other brainteaser she could find. When her event planning business got to be too much she brought me in and eventually handed the reins over when she decided to retire. She said it kept her mind sharp and given she died at ninety as quick as ever, who was I to argue?

When Aggie died, she left me her house as she and her late husband did not have any children. It was an old Victorian on a corner lot two blocks back from Main Street in Lake Wilson. Mitch had bought our old house from me, which struck me as odd. I would have thought that would make Heather uncomfortable, but it turned out she had been dying to gut and renovate it.

About two weeks ago, Mitch had come to me and offered to buy Aggie's place. I was shocked seeing as they had finally finished their renovations. He had made unconvincing arguments that it was a "family" home and should be passed down. Although, he wasn't the first member of the Brodsky clan to make that argument, I was convinced there was more to it in his case. Aggie's house would have had to be demoed to work for them.

"What offer?" Jess asked. I hadn't bothered to share his ridiculous offer since there were no conditions imaginable that would make me sell to him. And Jess was not Mitch's biggest fan so I didn't want to start a whole "what is he up to" discussion. Although, I did wonder what he was up to.

"No, I am not interested in selling. That is my final answer and you need to move on." I hated that he kept pushing until he got the answer he wanted. It was a major issue in our marriage and I didn't miss the tactic. In fact, these recent talks were reminders why I was at peace with our divorce.

"Yes, but I asked you to reconsider," he insisted.

I really don't get why NO is not understood to be a complete sentence. I think maybe to make it to the leve Mitch had in corporate America you just don't hear the word. But he should be used to hearing it from me by now. I was beginning to feel like I was talking to a toddler.

Jess started to look back and forth between us like she was attending a tennis match.

"One of the advantages of divorce is that I am no longer obligated to entertain reconsidering your offers, no matter how outlandish. I am not selling my house!" I responded louder than I meant. I hate feeling bullied and I certainly wasn't going to let him bully me on this. I really didn't want to lose it at an event I put together, but he was trying to take my home.

"He wants you to sell him your house?" Jess gasped. I nodded. She knew I loved that house and didn't love Mitch so it was a no brainer. She just shook her head.

"It's Aggie's and therefore a part of my family legacy." He really thought he was being reasonable. Now mind you, the man didn't want to send his family Christmas cards when we first got married because he claimed money was tight, but suddenly he expected me to turn over the keys to my house? The family legacy argument didn't have a ring of truth.

"She wanted me to have it," I repeated for the thousandth time. I swear I should tape this discussion and just hit replay next time he started talking to me.

"You know it should stay in the family," he repeated. At this point, he started looking down his nose at me as though being in the family was a privilege and I was somehow unworthy. Okay, maybe he was just standing and it looked that way, but it felt like he was looking down at me.

"Aggie never defined family by blood, and you know it. Besides, it was from her husband's family … one generation does not turn something into a family legacy. You really need to drop it. Especially here. This is neither the time nor the place. Besides, you don't have any need for it and she didn't even like you," I jabbed just a little below the belt.

"Aggie thought you were an ass, Mitch. She was bright that way," Jess confirmed, taking a bite of risotto. It really was good. I think I was more annoyed Mitch was interfering in my chance to indulge in gourmet food then the actual argument. A girl has to have priorities.

"If Aggie thought that it should stay in the family she would have left it to one of you. She didn't. This is why she had her competency certified by three experts at the time she signed her will. She figured one of you would push this. Besides, what do you want it for … you can't possibly need it?" I continued. Mitch's family wasn't as large as mine, but he still had cousins around who were never comfortable with me being named in Aggie's will.

"Heather wants it. For her business," he explained as though that cleared up everything. Now how that was supposed to explain anything I had no clue. Primarily because Heather (a) didn't have a business and (b) if she did, it couldn't possibly be for anything that needed a hundred-year-old Victorian home.

Jess snorted. And not the graceful kind of snort, either, if there is such a thing. We both turned and looked at her. I almost started laughing and then remembered I was supposed to be putting Mitch in his place.

"Are you out of your mind? That is your compelling reason? And since when does she have a business?" I asked pointedly. Nothing against Heather but her social calendar rivaled the Queen's so when she was going to fit work into it, I had no clue. Besides, she had dropped out of college five years ago when she married Mitch. Yeah, there's an age difference. The town's old biddies committee had a field day with that one.

"With the new vacation housing development, Lakeside Paradise, going up she is thinking of starting an interior design firm. She has a natural talent for it and a strong entrepreneurial spirit. The house would be a perfect office and showcase opportunity."

I spit out my drink. Those did not sound like Mitch's words. I felt like I just got a glimpse into Heather's pitch for the house. Either way, it hardly qualified as a compelling reason in my book.

"Did she go to school for that?" I asked. He just kept looking at me. "Well, get her an office space somewhere else. I'm not selling MY house and that is my final answer." The conversation was over and I broke eye contact with him. After all, asparagus wrapped in prosciutto was waiting.

He turned in a huff and left.

"Bye," Jess called out with way too much false charm, mumbling under her breath. I glanced over at her and noticed I had accidentally gotten rum and coke on her light blue dress when I snorted sometime during that ridiculous conversation. I felt terrible and immediately started blotting. She looked at me like I was some kind of crazy woman trying to cop a feel.

"I need to get my stain stick from the toolkit. That dress looks too good on you to ruin," I confessed, standing up. "Meet me in the bathroom in two minutes."

I always brought a bag with emergency necessities to every event. The "toolkit" as I called it contained Band-Aids, hairspray, shoelaces, assorted meds, breath mints, a flask, stain stick, Ziploc bags, condoms (don't ask), and anything else needed at the last minute. I kept the bag in the back utility closet where the extra linens and tableware supplies were kept when we had ballroom events. All the vendors used it. Luckily, it was just down the hall from the bathrooms, too.

I picked up my clutch and headed off to save the day.

Chapter Five

"Where are you off to in such a rush?" one of the groomsmen, Roger Atkins, asked me as I flew by. He was leaning against the bar with a brandy glass in his hand, obviously not his first drink of the night. "The happy couple is about to make their getaway. You should be heading out front with the masses."

Roger Atkins was Rodney Staltz's twin brother. Rodney changed his last name after their mother died his freshman year of college. He said he was very close to her and wanted to do something to honor her.

I restrained myself from asking why he wasn't out front if it was such a big deal. "Just need to visit the ladies room and I'll be right there. Hey, you wouldn't know where Rodney is, would you?" I asked. "He was supposed to be working here today."

"No, haven't seen him. Jess asked me earlier. I figured you guys fired him. Wouldn't have surprised me. This isn't his scene," Roger replied. True, it wasn't. But Rodney wasn't turning down any work if it got him closer to Nepal or Tibet or wherever monks lived.

I passed the bathroom doors on the left and turned right to make my way to the closet, feeling somewhat relieved. The happy couple was about to leave on their weekend getaway, clean up was beginning, and I was an hour away from twenty-four hours of rest and relaxation. As I approached the closet, I noticed a bracelet in the hallway outside the door and reached down to pick it up. I figured I would turn it in to the front desk on my way out to say goodbye to the happy couple.

Opening the door, I was immediately attacked by Rodney Staltz. Or I thought that was what was happening as I let out a loud scream. When I put my hands up and realized that he was stiff and falling, not attacking, I let out a much louder scream. I'm not going to lie, I was batting him away like something out of a bad toddler fight. I backed away enough that he landed with a thud on the ground.

When I finally looked down, I noticed the blood on his collar and the floor of the closet. I nudged his leg with my foot and then reached down to feel for a pulse just in case … Nothing. I had figured out what had happened to Rodney Staltz. He was dead and hiding in a closet.

Rodney was wearing a tuxedo and except for the whole dead eyes staring up he looked rather peaceful. I guess he had been leaning against the shelves on the right where the extra cherub centerpieces and the tablecloths were kept.

Huh, I thought we had three extra cherubs, but there are only two now. Weird.

I noticed my bag on the right set of shelves, but I wasn't going any further. In fact, I was going to get as far away as possible. But my eyes kept returning to the blood on the floor.

Turning around, I ran back toward the ballroom, but everyone had moved to the front of the resort to wave goodbye to Stacy and Carl. I quickly scanned the crowd looking for Scott Murphy, Jess's older brother. He was a member of the police department, like many on the guest list, and I knew he would be the one I should tell about my discovery. He wasn't hard to find, even from behind, standing next to who I assumed was the newest detective on our force since I hadn't been introduced to him yet.

"Hey, Scott, I kind of have an emergency," I blurted out. He and the man he was standing next to both turned and looked at me. Holy shit, it was Nick Carletti. When had he gotten back to town? And why hadn't anyone mentioned it? They both appeared to be in a good mood and enjoying the party. I hated that I was about to ruin all that but not much I could do. This wasn't exactly something that could wait.

"What's wrong, missing place setting?" Scott joked. He loved giving me a hard time. He'd been treating me like a younger sister since Jess and I became besties in kindergarten. I couldn't decide whether he made me glad or sad I was an only child.

"Um … no. I think I just found a dead body. In fact, I am pretty sure I did," I admitted. He and Nick both gave me their complete attention, all thought of the happy couple erased. "I was back in the utility closet getting something and Rodney Staltz is there … on the floor … in a pool of blood." Not my most articulate moment but I'm pretty sure they got the point.

Scott put his arm around me and started walking me back into the ballroom.

"Who is Rodney Staltz?" Scott asked.

"He's the guy who was supposed to be DJing the wedding. He never showed. We ended up having Carl's brother fill in." I looked up to see Nick was walking with us.

As we entered the ballroom, Scott walked me over to a table and sat down with me while Nick went back toward the closet.

Scott asked me if I was okay and just as I nodded Jess came out of the bathroom.

"Hey, Maddy, we are missing the big send off. What's the hold up?" Jess asked. She met my eyes and, realizing something was up, came over and wrapped me up in a hug. "What's wrong, hon?"

"Yeah, he's dead," Nick calmly stated as he returned from the hallway closet. He noticed Jess standing there and looked uncomfortable at dropping that bombshell. "Scott, call it in. I'll stay with the girls."

"Who is dead?" Jess asked Nick. She was rubbing my arms. I appreciated the comforting gesture.

"Rodney Staltz," I filled in as Nick took a seat next to me. Jess looked at me in shock. I think we were both thinking back to her words yesterday at The Dive. When she collected herself, Jess let Nick know the manager on duty would be the biggest help and then grabbed my hand. He got up, I assumed to go find the manager.

"Do you need anything?" Jess asked.

"No, but Jess, he's dead. What the hell? How did no one notice?"

The next thing I knew there was a brandy in front of me. I looked up to see Nick standing guard over us.

"Drink it. It will help warm you. I have to go make sure no one goes into the closet. Will you two be okay?" he asked. Nick was towering over us at six feet, two inches and he had kept in shape over the years. He had dark brown almost black hair with gray just starting at the temple. And his eyes were the same chocolate brown I remembered. I guess it's true that men get better looking with age.

"We'll be fine," Jess answered for the both of us. I wasn't sure I would go so far as to say fine, but I wasn't moving out of this chair anytime soon. Nick nodded and headed back to stand sentry until more officers arrived.

"When did Nick Carletti get back to town?" I asked her.

"Last week. He's the new detective working with Scott," she answered.

"And you didn't tell me because … ?" I asked.

"I was going to let it be a surprise. I thought you would see him tonight. I know how nervous you always got around him and I didn't want you being nervous today. Not with this wedding," she explained. Okay, that sort of made sense. And if I hadn't just found a dead body, I might appreciate it. But not so much now.

Jess instructed her staff to take care of the guests so she could stay with me. No one came into the ballroom that wasn't police personnel for the next hour. Scott and Nick eventually came back to us. Considering Scott's relationship with Jess, and by default me, it was agreed Nick would handle our statements.

"Jess, where were you while Maddy was going to the closet?" Nick asked.

"I was in the ladies room. We agreed to meet there to get a stain out of my dress," she replied.

"You didn't hear Maddy scream?" he asked.

"No, I mean, I guess my mind was just on everything I had to do to wrap up tonight."

"But you guys are still best friends, right? I mean, your best friend screams and you don't notice?" He was getting a little accusatory now.

"It's been a long week and I have a lot running through my head at the end of the night. I just was in my head," she explained.

He didn't look like he believed her, at least not entirely as he turned to me.

"So, tell me everything, Maddy, and take your time. Add anything, no detail is too small," he prompted. It was amazing how quickly he slipped into cop mode as he pulled out his notebook. Why would you bring a notebook to a wedding? I mean, did they have a manual that said always be prepared to take a murder witness's statement?

"Okay. I guess it starts with just before the reception. Jess and I were scrambling because Rodney hadn't shown. We both tried to call him. I tried every number I had for him. I left a message but never got a call back. I even called Tommy because he works at The Dive most nights," I started. I could already tell my babbling was going to take over.

"Tommy?" Nick asked.

"Tommy Stempler ... he owns The Dive. He was in my class in high school. Two years behind you," I explained. Scott and Nick had been juniors when Jess, Tommy, and I were freshman. I know Tommy and Nick played football together but I didn't think they were besties or anything.

"I remember."

"Anyway, Tommy hadn't heard from him so we just put a playlist on with Carl's brother handling the MC duties. Then about an hour ago, I spilled my drink on Jess's dress and went to get a stain stick. My toolkit was in the closet and ... "

"What's that?" Nick interrupted, pointing to my clutch. He really had to work on the rude thing.

"My clutch. The toolkit is a bag I bring to any event I work which has all kinds of things in it but it's hardly appropriate for carrying around," I explained. "So I went to get the stain remover and that's when I found Rodney."

"Was the door open or shut when you got there?" Nick continued. I appreciated him not going off on tangents.

"Shut. And I didn't move him or anything. I just nudged him. Oh, I did try to see if I could feel for a pulse." I knew enough not to go around touching everything and moving Rodney around once I figured he was dead. I wasn't a complete idiot.

"Nudged?" He looked confused. How was I supposed to know the technical term?

"You know, kicked with my foot. I guess I was hoping he was just hurt." I shrugged. I mean really, nudged was pretty self-explanatory. I looked at Jess for confirmation; I mean she got what I was saying.

Nick shook his head at me. I guess I would be more offended by his lack of professionalism if we hadn't gone to high school together and been in the same social circles. Our groups were always hanging out at Jess and Scott's house in one combination or another. Our school wasn't that big, and we always seemed to be at the same events. He was fond of torturing us almost as much as Scott was.

"Is there anything else? Anything odd about the night that stands out?" Nick asked.

"No, other than him being a no-show. Or what we thought was a no-show. The wedding was perfect," I replied.

"None of the staff reported anything odd. Although, I can ask around," Jess offered.

"No, that's our job," Nick answered. He turned to look at me. "You'll have to come down to the police station to sign this, but it can wait until tomorrow. Do you have a ride home? I don't think you should be driving yourself." He almost sounded genuinely concerned. I probably should have appreciated it more, but I honestly just wanted to get out of there.

"We'll make sure she gets home," Jess said.

"Call me tomorrow before you come to make sure I'm at the station. We can go over your statement and anything you might want to add," he said as he handed me his card. "My cell number is on the card, too. We're taking your bag into evidence for the time being, but I'll try to see if I can get it released to you then." Nick got up and went back to work.

"Rob will drive you home. I called him and he's on his way. I don't want you driving," Jess said.

"No argument here." I wasn't up for it, either. "Wait, did someone let Tommy know?"

"I'll handle it. I just want to get you home right now. Don't worry about any of that."

"Jess, should we tell them?" I asked. I hoped she knew what I meant. I didn't really want to say it out loud.

"What? About what I said yesterday? That was heat of the moment. I wasn't serious," she answered.

"I know that. Scott would know that. But Nick hasn't been back here in years and I don't want someone else mentioning it," I explained.

"No, if it comes up, I'll just explain. I mean, me killing someone? It's ridiculous."

There was really nothing else for me to do. Rob drove me home. I reassured Jess I didn't need company for the night and changed into a sleep shirt. How had a wedding, something I had done literally hundreds of times, turn into a murder? And Rodney? I mean, Jess's outburst aside yesterday, I don't think I had heard a single bad word said about him. When he moved to town in high school there was the usual distrust of the new people adjustment,

27

but everyone got over that. And I know he had been in trouble, but I didn't know how well known that had been. Although, I guess now I had to wonder.

I was convinced I would never get to sleep but I guess the adrenaline rush was over. I tossed in bed for a while before finally drifting off.

Chapter Six

Sunday

I woke the next morning a little confused. My first reaction was surprise that I woke before my alarm. I almost never do that on a yoga day. Then last night came flooding back in a rush. I remembered I hadn't set my usual yoga class alarm figuring I would be in no mood to clear my mind and downward dog today. And I was right. I had discovered a dead body last night and it was just hitting me what that meant. Rodney was dead. I had seen him at The Dive, in yoga, and had talked to him some about the wedding. I knew he liked music, could mix a drink, and was by far the best yoga student I had ever seen. I knew he had family in town but also knew he wasn't that close to Roger. His mother had died a few years ago of cancer. I almost felt guilty for the mental tongue-lashing I had given him yesterday when he hadn't shown for the wedding.

There was no use lying in bed all day so I made my way down to the kitchen for a Diet Coke and a bagel. I really wasn't equipped to make much more. I couldn't get his face out of my mind. Would it have been easier if his eyes had been closed? I was sure it was a completely normal reaction but that was hardly comforting. Why was he in the closet? None of his equipment was being stored there. He was using the resort's equipment so all he had to bring was himself and maybe a computer. The days of lugging records went out with my eighth-grade dances. So how did he end up in the closet? And who would want to harm him? I mean, he seemed pretty harmless.

The first time I met Rodney was when he walked into Cousin Cathy's yoga class. A man joining our group was usually news but a man we hadn't seen in years … stop the presses. Turns out he had just moved back to town and had been looking for a practice to join. I think calling Cousin Cathy's yoga classes a "practice" was a stretch, but he was pretty serious about his yoga. The next time I saw him was at The Dive. Tommy had hired him as a bartender. He seemed quiet and unassuming but friendly enough. I wondered if Tommy knew more about him?

My phone dinged pulling me out of my thoughts. Jess was texting to let me know she had to go to the resort for a meeting with her boss. I'm guessing dead bodies didn't look good on brochures, so they probably wanted to do damage control. Better her than me. She was good at that kind of thing. That was the story of our lives … opposites in almost every way.

My new wonderings were interrupted by another text letting me know we were having dinner at The Dive to talk. I probably could have predicted that if I were on my A game today. But I was going to be lucky if I got to my B game by the time we had dinner tonight. Oh no … Tommy. I wondered how he was doing. Not that he and Rodney were great friends, but someone should check up on him. Ughh … they really needed to come up with handbook for this kind of thing.

I shot him off a text, but knowing Tommy he would wait until we came in tonight before saying anything. If I needed him he would be there, but he wasn't going to butt in if he wasn't called. Chances were Jess had already filled him in on every detail anyway.

I finished my bagel and decided I might as well be semi-productive. There was dry cleaning I had to drop off, vendor checks to deliver, and a witness statement to sign. *Which of these does not belong?* Entering my dream master bath, the first remodel I had done on Aunt Aggie's, I gasped when I caught my reflection in the mirror. I looked like I had gone ten rounds with Rocky. My hair was sticking up in all directions, I had raccoon eyes from mascara, and I just looked lost, for lack of a better word. This is why they tell you to take your makeup off before going to bed. After a long shower where I started to feel human again, I changed into comfy jeans and a gray polo and started gathering the dry cleaning. When I got to the pants I wore last night, I noticed there was something in the pocket and pulled out the bracelet I had found outside the closet. *Damn … I probably should have given this to Nick.* It was a delicate gold bracelet and it spelled out SARAH in cursive.

The only Sarah I knew was Sarah Stevens, one of the bridesmaids. But what would Sarah's bracelet be doing there? I supposed it could have been there for a few days or even weeks, although they did regularly use the hallway so I would think someone would have found it before me. And it was still shiny, not dull as you would expect something that had been there for a while would be. Either way, I was pretty sure Nick would not be happy I forgot to hand it over.

I took the dry cleaning down, trying not to kill myself on the stairs. Gracefulness was not in my wheelhouse. I put the bracelet in a plastic bag (I had watched enough *CSI*), found Nick's card, and entered his contact info in my phone … business habit. I called him and left a message that I would be at the police department around 2 p.m., then I grabbed the vendor checks and headed out. I should have been able to make it to the police department sooner, but I already knew word of the death would have spread around town and I was going to have to answer the same questions at every stop. Small town predictability could be comforting, but it could also be annoying.

Getting in the car, I put on some Manilow and prepared to be grilled by some of the best interrogators in the business … small town neighbors who "just wanted to make sure I was okay." It was a good thing we were meeting at The Dive tonight; I was going to need a drink. Or ten.

Chapter Seven

One of the few advantages of having told my story over and over and over again for the last few hours was the amount of detail I recalled now. Maybe this should be a new police investigation tool. Have half the shop owners in a town quiz you for four hours. I was feeling pretty confident I knew what I had seen when I walked into the LWPD at 2:15 p.m. to meet with Nick. I had texted I would be a little late because Mrs. Murphy, Jess's mom, insisted on a second cup of tea after such a "harrowing experience," her words not mine.

"I'm here to see Detective Carletti," I politely informed the desk sergeant. He looked like something out of central casting. His nametag said PARKER and I thought I recognized the name, but not him. His uniform was starched within an inch of its life and his hairline had disappeared years ago.

"Is he expecting you?" he asked.

"I am. I'll take her back, Dan. Thanks," Nick interrupted as he emerged from the office door and gave a nod to Dan. Dan Parker, now I remembered. There was a Parker on the high school baseball team when MJ played. That must have been Dan's son. Nick walked me back to an empty room with a table and chairs on each side. I wondered if this was an interrogation room, if that's what they called them.

"Here's your bag. It doesn't look like we will need it so you can take it with you." He handed it to me across the table once we were both seated. His suit looked crisp, but I could tell he had already put in a long day. He was one of those who wore their stress on their face.

"How did you sleep?" Nick asked before taking a sip of coffee he had brought in.

"Actually, I kind of crashed. I'm sure I dreamt about it but I don't remember anything. Probably an adrenaline crash. I mean, I would think it was that. I was staring into space for a while but then I was out. No tossing or turning. No mindless roaming an empty house, just peaceful sleep," I explained needlessly. What was it about him that had me babbling? I had known him all my life and he had pretty much made me nervous since middle school. At least that was when "the crush" as Jess and Tommy liked to call it started.

That's right. The main attraction in all my high school happily ever after fantasies was now sitting across from me and asking about a dead body that had fallen on me. Not that I imagined seeing him after all these years, but this was certainly not how I had pictured it. There had always been something about Nick Carletti that held my attention. I could get lost in his eyes for hours. Or at least I thought I could. Not that I ever got the chance. But I always wondered what it would be like to just be allowed to look at him. Now it just seemed like I was a stalker.

Nick opened the folder on the table and handed me a typed copy of my statement before asking me to review it for accuracy. I read it and then looked up. While he was looking down at the folder, I got a good look at him. In all honesty, he hadn't changed that much since high school. He still looked like a mischievous little boy who was living in an adult body. The kind of guy who would volunteer for the dunk tank at a church fair only to haze those throwing the baseballs.

"Maddy, I do have a couple of questions."

"Okay, what do you need?"

"I know you were working last night, but at any time did you notice Jess was absent for a prolonged period?" Well, I guess I knew where this was going.

"Prolonged period?"

"Yeah, was there any time when you didn't know where she was?"

"I wasn't exactly looking for her often. I mean, it was my job to make sure any issues were handled quickly. I don't do the hostess side at something like this, I do the fixing someone's meal kind of thing. But to answer your question, no. There was never a time when I looked for her that I couldn't find her." And that was true. Although, I don't know that I looked for her at all really. I mean, we had it down to a science after all these years. But that is not what Nick asked.

"So you never noticed her missing?"

"No. She was working the biggest event of the year. She wasn't going to wander off."

"Right, the biggest event where the victim had ditched her."

"Okay, first of all, he didn't ditch her. It wasn't her wedding. Second, we handled it. And after we fixed it we moved on." I mean really, no one kills someone over missing a gig.

"But she did have an issue with Rodney's absence the day before … correct?"

"Well, she wasn't happy about it. But she talked to him and he promised to be there. It was handled." I didn't like where he was going with this. I would be the first to admit that Rodney had ticked off Jess by missing the run through and maybe she didn't pick the best phrasing to express her displeasure, but he had to know Jess wasn't capable of murder. Not over this.

"Okay, anything else?" Nick asked.

"Um … there are a few things to add, I guess," I started sheepishly. I reached into my purse and pulled out the baggie with the bracelet and slid it over to him. He picked it up and began to study it.

"What's this?" he asked, eyebrow raised. No matter how many times I rehearsed it this next sentence wasn't going to sound good. Might as well just rip the Band-Aid off.

"Well, I sort of found it in the hallway to the closet when I first walked in. I picked it up thinking I would turn it in to Jess for lost and found. But then I found Rodney and I guess I totally forgot about it until this morning as I was getting the dry cleaning ready."

"You forgot you picked this up?" I suddenly felt like I was being questioned by my dad. I wonder if that tone of voice was a prerequisite. His mom, who owned Slice of Heaven, mentioned he had two daughters who were in college or maybe one was still attending and one had graduated? He had divorced a few years ago. I wondered if he was dating anyone now. Jess said he had just returned to town but the single women in our town were not known for patience. Present company excluded of course.

"In my defense it wasn't evidence when I picked it up. And it's not every day you discover your first dead body. It just slipped my mind. It's not

34

like I meant to forget it," I said defensively. I realized then and there I would probably never be able to lie to Nick. Not that I planned on it but there was something about his eyes that just made it impossible. I mean, who could look at those eyes and lie?

"Fine. Anything else?" he inquired. I noticed he was a little more focused now that he realized I may be adding information to my statement.

"A few things I remember," I admitted. "We originally ordered three extra cherub centerpieces from Kay Morgan. But when I opened the closet door, I noticed that there were only two left. Jess or I would be the only ones to retrieve them and I know I didn't so you should ask her. And I think there was a tablecloth missing from the shelf. When I put my bag in there that morning there were three equal piles but when I found the body one of the piles was missing a tablecloth. Not sure if that matters, but you asked," I ended.

"So a missing angel and tablecloth? And who is Kay Morgan?" he asked as he finished noting in his book.

"Kay is the florist the Barton's used for the wedding. She is also Lucy Barton's best friend. And it was a cherub, not an angel," I corrected. He looked up at me like I was crazy. "Well, there is a difference. A cherub is a type of angelic being. It's like the difference between a condiment and ketchup. Also, traditionally cherubs directly serve God while angels are an intermediary between gods and mortals. So, they are kind of different."

"You always were a stickler for language. Is that all?" he asked. I couldn't figure out if he was impatient with me or life in general, but I was starting to take this personally.

"I'm not a stickler, I just appreciate accuracy. Listen, you asked me if there was anything else. It isn't my fault there is," I said. Although, I guess technically it could be considered my fault I didn't remember all of this last night.

"I know. I'm sorry. I'm running on too much coffee and too little sleep. And you have been helpful." He relaxed a little. "Especially the cherub part. The victim died of blunt force trauma to the back of the head. The missing cherub could explain the lack of an obvious weapon. And that is not for public consumption." He looked at me pointedly. I think he realized he said more than he should. "Who picked those out anyway? They could give a person nightmares."

"Lucy Barton," I answered quickly, feeling vindicated about the cherubs.

"We don't know much about the victim," he continued, and it suddenly occurred to me he didn't really care who picked out the cherubs.

"Well, he moved back to town a while ago, worked at The Dive as a bartender but didn't drink, was a serious yoga practitioner, an avid reader, liked to paint, and was a vegan. And he lived in an apartment on Elm," I offered. "Also, he had family here, a twin brother … Roger Atkins. Although, I'm not sure how close they were. 'Different life journeys,' is how he phrased it. I got the impression they were opposites. I always thought twins were close, but I guess not." I smiled triumphantly.

"Where did you get all this?" Nick asked while making notes. Oh, how quickly people forget when they've lived in the big city for years. Small town gossip was alive and well in the twenty-first century and apparently Nick had forgotten that little fact.

"You grew up here, you know better than anyone how this town works. I've been talking to everyone non-stop for the last four hours. I'm surprised I don't have his social security number. I also talked to him after yoga every week, and Tommy hired him and filled me in. I think Tommy knows more about his background. I kind of got the impression Rodney just wanted a quiet life," I added.

"I can understand that given his last address," he stated cryptically. It was my turn to raise an eyebrow at what he meant by that. Although, my eyebrow was nowhere near as lethal as his. It made sense Nick would know Rodney served time, but I just didn't see him as being a criminal mastermind or vicious murderer. He seemed so meek, but I had to admit my experience with criminals was somewhat limited, as far as I knew.

"Thanks for coming in and getting this taken care of. And I appreciate you adding what you remembered to the statement." He was obviously ending the interview.

"Oh, Roger was near the bar before I went back to the closet. He was getting a refill before the sendoff. Probably because they were closing down the bar," I suddenly remembered.

"Is that all now?" he pressed, obviously exasperated, But he seemed less annoyed with me now then at the beginning of the interview. I guess being helpful pays off.

"Yeah, that is all I can remember. And I didn't get to say it at the wedding but welcome back to town. I'm sure Scott is glad to have you on the force and back home. I know he's had to carry a lot of the load by himself since the last detective retired. Not that Lake Wilson is a huge hot bed of crime. But it seemed to be wearing on him," I added, no clue why I was babbling again.

"Yeah, I needed a change from the city," he muttered. Now that was vague.

"Well, let me know if you need anything else," I said while heading out. I grabbed my purse and toolkit bag, walking in front of him on our way to the front.

"Maddy, just don't get too involved. I remember you were always reading mysteries and working on puzzles. And I wouldn't want you getting stuck in any more lockers. This is serious and you should leave it to us," he warned as he walked me out to the door. Of course, he would remember that. Get stuck in one locker and no one ever forgets it.

"Finding his body was more than enough. Investigating is your specialty not mine," I replied. And I swear, at that moment I meant it.

Chapter Eight

I had time to spare until I met Jess so I figured I would go home and check email. I had converted the study on the first floor of the house into my home office. It looked out over the back garden and had plenty of natural light, which I preferred. I had exchanged Aggie's Victorian themed furniture for a functional L-desk and Herman Miller office chair. Expensive but worth every penny. I also added a reading chair by the back windows. It was great for napping. Not that I would ever skip work for sleep. But, you know, studies show power naps lead to increased productivity.

I checked my email and found mostly quick response work related messages. My next event, an anniversary dinner, was pretty much under control, and everything after that was on track. Anything directly related to a client I decided to save for tomorrow. I wasn't ready to deal with Mrs. Ryerson's suggestion of a belly dancer at her mother's seventy-fifth birthday party yet.

I also had emails from the kids. Mostly updates. MJ was working on a Churchill tank restoration. He had an internship at a British museum as part of his graduate schoolwork and he tended to get technical, so I glossed over to where he was telling me he was healthy and happy. He was the epitome of low maintenance.

Megan's was a little longer. She gave me the standard work update and then launched into a review of a bunch of new recipes she had tried. She loved cooking and had just converted to vegan, so I had months of reviews to look forward to. But she ended with "Call me" so I was intrigued.

Megan was my oldest at twenty-six and lived in California. If I was honest, she was more like Mitch than me when it came to demeanor. But the stubbornness was all mine. I would have loved to have her closer, but she was happy out there. I checked the time and realized that even with the three-hour west coast time difference she would be at work. I found her work contact and hit send.

"This is Megan," she picked up on the second ring. I could picture her at her keyboard with computer screens taking up most of her attention.

"This is your mother. Just got your email, what's up kiddo?" I knew she had me on speaker and was never sure who was around, so I always tried to keep from being embarrassing when I called.

"Hey, Mom. I just wanted to talk to you about a guy I met but then Cousin Carrie texts me this morning asking if I had heard from you because she was concerned for your aura after FINDING A DEAD BODY! Wanna tell me why I had to hear about it from Cousin Tea Leaf?" she demanded. I hope she had a closed office otherwise her co-workers were going to think I was a nut job.

"I was going to email you and your brother, but I have just been busy. Besides, I just found him ... I didn't do it or anything," I explained. I mean, really, in the big picture I wasn't that involved. I don't know why I was being defensive. I was the parent after all.

"You had to know someone was going to tell us. I just would have preferred to hear it from you. Are you okay? That must have been horrible." She had forgiven my faux pas pretty quickly. But she was right.

"Yes, I'm fine. I didn't know the victim that well so that probably helped." I hoped that didn't sound too callus. I didn't want her to worry, and I was kind of done with this particular topic of conversation for right now. And it's not like she or MJ could have done anything. I didn't want them thinking they had to rush home to comfort me or any of that crap.

"Good, I guess. Is that what you say in this situation? And just to make sure you don't make the same mistake again, I assured Carrie you would be in for an aura cleanse this week," she smirked through the phone. That she got from me, too. Cousin Carrie was pretty sure everyone needed an aura cleanse on a regular basis.

"Gee ... thanks. Remind me you deserve coal this year. Anyhow, let's get back to the guy you mentioned in your email. Who is he? And have you told your brother?" I asked. Megan was not a serial dater so if she mentioned this one then she must be interested. I didn't think she "needed" a man to be happy, but I wanted both kids to have someone to share their lives with. Although, I was in no way, shape, or form ready to be a grandmother, thank you very much.

"He's a personal chef and we just had a couple of dates. I'm holding off telling MJ. You know how protective he is. I don't need him flying halfway around the world to give my date the third degree. Sometimes I think he forgets I'm the older sibling," she said.

"I know. But you're his big sister and can do no wrong. He would do anything for you, so quit your whining," I teased. I would have to make a point not to mention it to MJ for at least a couple of emails.

"So, what did he say about you finding dead bodies?" she pushed.

Since I didn't have a good answer I figured my best bet would be to just pretend I didn't hear the question. Not like it was going to work, but there were no good choices.

"You didn't tell him, did you?" she continued. "You're lucky he's too busy with his toys to pay attention to text messages. You should at least text him to let him know. He always reads your messages first. And as curious as he is about 1942 and dead people, he won't care about Joe Schmoe the corpse." That's true. Rodney hadn't been dead long enough to be considered "historic" or interesting to MJ.

"He does? Aww ... I knew he was my favorite," I joked. "Stop making fun of your brother. Not everyone can be a science head. The world needs history majors, too, you know," I defended. As a fellow history major, it was my job to stand up for MJ.

"I know. I'm actually thinking about going to visit him. We'll have to see how work goes." The one thing I had done right was my kids and it thrilled me to no end that they loved each other even without me prodding.

"Okay, I have to go get ready for dinner with Jess and Tommy. Let me know how your next date goes," I nagged.

"How do you know there is another date planned?" she asked.

"Mother's intuition. You wouldn't have mentioned him otherwise. Love you. Talk to you soon," I said, sensing I had gotten as much out of her as I could.

"Love you, too, Mom," she responded. I could tell I had lost her attention and she was back to the world of zeros and ones.

Ending the call, I sent a text off to MJ since it was late in England and he was probably already asleep. I knew by now to start with "I'm fine." The details wouldn't interest him but at least Cousin Carrie wouldn't be scheduling me for a double header.

Chapter Nine

The good thing about meeting at The Dive is that no matter what I was wearing I was perfectly dressed. Since I was planning on having a drink or two, I decided to walk. I only lived a couple of blocks from Main St. and it was one block down on the right from there. By time I walked in, I was only five minutes late so Jess was already at our table with our first round. Tommy waved to me from behind the bar and put up two fingers meaning he would join us in a minute. I sat down in the rounded both and ever so not gracefully scooted into the middle. From there we could see everything.

The Dive was actually not that much of one. When Tommy bought it ten years ago it had been, but he had slowly classed it up some. The bar, which was of course the centerpiece, had been restored and even had traditional brass accents. Glassware hung from ceiling holders and the mirrored backing gave the impression the bar was larger than it actually was. There were doors on either side, one leading to the bathrooms and the other to the kitchen.

Our booth was in the corner. It was hidden from the windows but still allowed us to look out. It also allowed Tommy to join us but keep an eye on the place, so nothing got out of control. Since it was Sunday night, it wasn't that crowded. Football season would have been a different story, but we had a few months till then. There were probably only half a dozen tables occupied as I looked around.

"So how did it go at the station?" I asked Jess as Tommy came over with his Blue Moon and joined us. Tonight, I had a margarita on the rocks with no salt and Jess had her signature Malibu Bay Breeze. Tommy said he could always tell by how we looked when we came in what we needed to drink, and he was right tonight. I took my first sip and consciously relaxed my shoulders.

"Not great. I think Nick is seriously thinking of me as a suspect. Can you believe it? I don't need this on top of dealing with the damage control at The Resort," Jess said. "I missed most of the excitement and wasn't with you when you found Rodney. I mean, I did see him talking with Jean-Paul earlier and it appeared to be heated, but for all I know they were discussing their favorite cheeses. I didn't actually hear them. But that was it. I didn't see him after that. He needs to be looking at someone else, anyone else," she said.

"I'm sure Nick will realize you had nothing to do with it soon enough," I said reaching out and giving her a side hug.

"I hope so. I mean, I was running around checking on food and everything else. I was too busy to kill anyone." As much as she was trying to brush it off I could tell Nick's suspicions were really scaring her. Our lives were relatively boring so being considered a murder suspect was a big shock to the system.

"Yeah, that reminds me, I need Jean-Paul's contact info. The food was amazing. Actually, what I need to do is talk to him about my Ryerson party. Think you could arrange that since I didn't talk to him much?" I asked as I reached for my phone hoping she would take the hint to send his information now. There's no need to be subtle between friends.

"No problem." She immediately shared his contact information. "I might steer clear of any Rodney talk if I were you. It was kind of obvious they didn't get along."

"Did you mention the argument to Nick?" I asked.

"Yeah, I did. I felt guilty doing it, but he asked what I saw and I told him. That doesn't make me a snitch does it? Snitches get stitches. I don't want to be a snitch."

"No, I'm pretty sure you are clear on that. I am curious, what were they arguing about? I got the impression Rodney didn't know that many people in town. And how would he have upset Jean-Paul?" I just couldn't see them crossing paths.

"Well, Jean-Paul never comes in here and Rod never mentioned him," Tommy said. "Rod spent most of his spare time meditating and painting. Those were the only things he ever discussed. He was thinking of looking into moving to an artist commune in Nepal or something. I mean, really, he was the definition of harmless," Tommy added. "And I may need you to fill in a night or two, Mads, just until I find someone." If he had asked I would have tried to get out of it but since he didn't ask I couldn't said no. Tommy logic for you

When I was in college, I took a bartending class when I was bored one semester. My mom thought it would help me make friends. When Tommy bought The Dive, he decided that made me a qualified fill-in for his staff.

"No clue why they would argue. You know chefs," Jess shrugged, "they are passionate and temperamental. Maybe it was nothing. Anyway, I'll set up the appointment. The food really was out of this world, wasn't it? He's not hot headed like a lot of chefs. But he puts on a fake accent. Not really sure what it's supposed to be, he's probably from Kansas or something. But if he can make Lucy happy then he can handle any job." Jess held up her glass for a salute and I mirrored her.

It wouldn't be overly dramatic to say the wedding was one of the more stressful events in my career. Lucy Barton could have done real damage to my business if she was unhappy. Her family had been in this town since the Mayflower and her husband, though a newer transplant, was very influential. If Lake Wilson had a power couple, they would be considered it. I was just relieved she didn't seem to be blaming the murder for ruining the reception. I think it had a lot to do with the fact everyone had pretty much left or was on their way out by then. They had closed the open bar when the bride and groom left so no one was coming back when the police closed the ballroom off.

"Lucy actually called me this morning," Jess continued. "She was sort of basking at being the center of attention. She claimed everyone was calling asking her how she was after such a trauma. You would have thought she came upon the murder in action. Anyway, she was impressed with how The Resort handled it. She was worried it would have been a scandal, but everyone seems to be thinking of the murder as an after party as opposed to part of the main event," she explained.

"Just so long as she's not running around ruining us she can claim what she wants," I said. Finding another career at this point in my life was not something I was eager to start. I was lucky enough to fall into this one and it fit. I wouldn't even begin to know where to go if I had to start over.

"What about you? How was your interview with Nick?" Jess asked. I could have sworn she added a singsong tone like we were in high school again. I really was hoping she forgot the crush I used to have on him, but it appeared

44

it was front and center in her memory bank.

"Fine, although he could be a little annoyed with me now," I admitted. That got me an eyebrow raise. I was getting sick of those today. "I sort of picked a bracelet up from the closet and took it home. Forgot about it until this morning. So I guess leaving with evidence is not the way to ingratiate yourself to the newest detective. I think I redeemed myself by realizing one of the cherubs was missing."

"It was? Who the hell would take one of those evil creatures?" she wondered.

"No clue. Although, Nick thinks they are evil, too," I finished before taking another sip of my margarita. There really were very few things that tasted better than a well-made margarita after finding a body. Not that I had a ton of experience, but you get the idea.

"Evil cherubs?" Tommy asked. He hadn't been on the guest list so this was all news to him.

"Karen and Lucy picked these large glass cherubs for the centerpieces for the guests' tables. We had extras in the utility closet. Anyway, one of them was missing when I went into the closet," I explained to Tommy. Just then, Kyle came out to drop off potato skins and wings for the table. "Hey, Cuz, how are your parents?" I asked while reaching for a potato skin. Kyle was one of my cousins, although I'm not really sure how the whole second cousin once removed thing worked, so we all just used Cousin. Kyle was on my dad's side, he was my cousin Shane's son and was working part time for Tommy.

"They are doing good, thanks. Gotta get back to the kitchen. Boss is a real slave driver," he winked to Tommy. Most people didn't want to get between the three of us when we were huddled together with food. And I couldn't blame them. I was known for my love of the perfect food ... the potato skin. Tommy knew to order them with extra cheese, just the way I liked them. The wings were for Tommy and Jess. I couldn't do spicy, and they loved extra hot wings. It literally hurt to watch them go to town on them. I tried them once and couldn't feel my lips for three days. No, thank you.

"And they really were creepy," Jess continued a couple of minutes later as she picked up a wing and drenched it in ranch. She should probably just drink it by the glass.

"What were?" Tommy asked, already having moved on from the topic. He was a blue cheese and wing purist. It was one of the few unhealthy things he ate.

"The cherubs ... keep up," I winked. Jess was like a dog with a bone and Tommy had the attention span of a kindergartener if it wasn't business related. "And she's right ... they were creepy. But that's what Lucy wanted so that's what we got. Anyway, there was one missing when I found Rodney. Did you take it for some reason?" I asked Jess. She shook her head while digging into her third wing.

Hmmm ... they were kind of heavy, the cherubs, not the wings. And if you lifted one over your head and brought it down it could do some serious damage. What a way to die, bludgeoned by a glass cherub. But how do you just walk out with a bloody statute and no one notice?

"So, what about the bracelet?" Jess pressed on.

"It was a thin gold bracelet. It had SARAH spelled out. The only Sarah I remember at the wedding was the bridesmaid Sarah Stevens but I can't see why she would have been near the closet. And I didn't see her go back there, but that doesn't mean anything since it's not like I was watching the hallway. Although, I'm pretty sure she's never so much as stepped on an ant let alone bashed someone over the head with a cherub," I answered.

"It's always the quiet ones who turn out to be serial killers. Besides, remember how jumpy she was at the rehearsal dinner? She dropped that glass of wine and it almost splashed on Lucy's shoes. Then we would have had a front row seat to a murder," Jess replied. She was pointing a chicken wing in a dangerous manner. If I ended up with hot sauce on my shirt, I was not going to look for stain remover tonight. I had learned my lesson. But she was right. Sarah had dropped a glass of red wine during the mingle portion of the rehearsal dinner while talking to other members of the wedding party. I wasn't paying enough attention to her to tell if she was jumpy but that is the kind of thing Jess would notice.

"Well, there is another person Rod didn't get along with," Tommy piped up. We both turned to look at him. "Rod's brother Roger came in and they definitely argued. It was a few nights ago. It was the only time I have seen Rod upset or even animated for that matter. Not sure what it was about but he told Roger he wasn't going to let him do it again, whatever that means," he said, taking a sip of beer. Only Tommy would drop something like that and move on to his beer.

"Hmmm ... makes you wonder," I thought out loud.

"NO!!" they both said in unison. You would have thought I just suggested pole dancing in Antarctica the way they both jumped in.

"What? I'm just saying," I said, shrugging my shoulders innocently.

"You are not playing Nancy Drew," Tommy responded. "This is a real murder and he's really dead." I so wanted to point out the redundancy but let it slide. See, not so much of a stickler.

"I'm just saying that maybe this is a little more interesting than I first thought ... that's all," I directed at him. "Besides, where is the harm in thinking? I mean, I can't help it if there are questions that need answering." I don't think he was buying it.

"Do you not remember Maddy Carson and the Case of the Missing Spanish Test?" Tommy asked.

"That was years ago! Besides, that was totally different," I replied. Although, I wasn't sure it really was. During our sophomore year of high school, Mrs. Rodrigo's Spanish II mid-term had gone missing. It was a big deal in a small school. I was convinced I knew who took it. I had seen Rupert Franz and his friends outside her classroom the afternoon it was taken, and everyone knew he struggled with language classes. It's why in his senior year he was on his third language. So, one day I hid in the boy's locker room so I could go through his locker while he was at football practice. Except I sort of got stuck in a locker, totally not my fault, and Nick found me when practice was over. And he was wrapped in a towel from having showered. I ended up looking like a peeping tom. I guess I should be happy it was the 80s and all I got was detention.

"No, there are questions the cops need answered ... not you. We do not need another Peeping Maddy fiasco," Jess added her two cents. I could tell she was wavering though. She was just as curious as I was, and besides, she didn't appreciate the police suspecting her of the murder. And it's not like I was suggesting anything. I just thought it was interesting what you could learn by asking a few simple questions. I mean, twenty-four hours ago I couldn't imagine anyone wanting to hurt Rodney and now it turns out two people had argued with him and one person appeared to be somewhere they shouldn't have been.

Besides, my best friend was still on the list of suspects and I could tell it was bothering her. If I could take this off her plate, wasn't it my duty?

"Speaking of cops," I decide a change of topic was due, "how does your brother feel about Nick being back? I mean, I know the chief is retiring soon. Does Scott want the job?" I could be a master deflector when needed. Besides, I knew Scott and Nick used to be close and if they were going to be friends again job tension could be a real problem.

"We're not done with the Rod topic. But Scott is thrilled Nick is back. Being the only detective was wearing on him. And he never wanted the chief's job, he hates the political side. I did ask him if Nick wanted it and he think he does. That would be great for Scott, actually, so I'm kind of hoping Nick gets it. So long as he doesn't arrest me for murder." I knew she would have asked already. And she was right that Scott wasn't made for politics. He loved being a cop, but he didn't love the paperwork and administrative side. Now that I thought about it, being chief would be a nightmare for him. But would it be any better for Nick? I knew he'd been gone a while but I didn't remember him being particularly good at politics.

"Speaking of not being good at things," Tommy started, "I need a favor." Okay, this was interesting.

"Sure," Jess and I replied like the Doublemint Twins.

"Tomorrow is my anniversary with Mateo. He mentioned liking one of Rod's paintings one day and I hired him to do one of our place on the lake. I was supposed to pick it up today, but the cops just released the apartment before you guys got here and I haven't been able to pick it up. I'm picking Mateo up right after closing and we are spending the day at the lake tomorrow. Anyway, can one of you pick it up at Rod's and bring it out for me? I'm trying to surprise him, and I can't figure out a way to get it without making him suspicious."

"Awww," we had this Doublemint thing down. Tommy wasn't an openly romantic kind of guy. PDAs were never his thing, but he was really good at the grand romantic gestures. Mateo was going to love this.

"Sure, I'll get it tomorrow morning and bring it out," I volunteered. The beauty of being your own boss was you could be late to work.

"Great, here's the key. You can just leave it on the porch tomorrow morning. Mat gets to pick what we are doing so I have no clue if we'll be there. You're a life saver." He kissed my cheek as he got up and reached in his pocket and took a key off his ring. "It's the Elm Street house, unit #3," Tommy added. He owned half the apartment buildings in town. Most were old homes he bought, restored, and subdivided. Anything resembling an apartment complex was outside of town or at the lake itself. The historical society had worked hard to make sure as many homes in town kept their original charm.

"I have to head home," Jess said, while getting up from the table, too. "Kids have school tomorrow and I have to be at the office early. We have a staff meeting on how to 'handle' the whole Rodney dead body thing." I couldn't imagine a meeting on how to handle the discovery of a murdered body at your resort. Again, handbooks would be helpful. Just as we hugged Rob came in to pick Jess up. I refused the offer for a ride; it was too nice a night.

I took my time walking home, wondering how someone who was as quiet and as unassuming as Rodney could have ended up murdered at the biggest wedding of the year and no clear motive for killing him. I mean, if he had a reputation for something then maybe it would make sense. But until today I thought Rodney was a blend into the surroundings kind of guy. Nothing stood out about him. But now I had to wonder what else it was we didn't know about him.

Chapter Ten

Monday

The next morning, I found myself up bright and early in front of Rodney's apartment door. I couldn't seem to shut my mind off last night. Every time I closed my eyes, I saw his body there on the hallway floor. And when I gave up trying to sleep and just stared into the dark, I kept wondering what could possibly have driven someone to take his life. It's not that we didn't have crime in Lake Wilson, but such a senseless act of violence was rare. I couldn't help but wonder if the police had any suspects other than Jess.

I used the key Tommy gave me to enter Rodney's apartment. His unit was in a renovated Victorian house Tommy bought a couple of years ago. He subdivided the inside into four one-bedroom apartments. Rodney's was located on the second floor. After entering through what was once the house's front door there was a large center staircase leading up. I checked the mailbox near the front door and grabbed Rodney's mail. I was kind of surprised the police hadn't emptied it but it wasn't exactly a goldmine: an ad for the local grocery store, a cell phone bill, and a postcard for a cleaning service. Going up to the second floor, Rodney's apartment was on the left. There was a welcome mat out front that looked new. I let myself in and was somewhat surprised how neat and airy it was.

The apartment was an open kitchen/dining/living room floor plan with a door off to the left, which I assumed was the bedroom. There were plenty of windows and the blinds were all open. A comfortable sofa, coffee table, and small stereo made up the living room. There was no television or computer, which I found odd. The bookshelf contained vegan cookbooks, yoga guides, art guides, and a lot of meditation resources. Most seemed to be borrowed from the library. *Note to self: make sure Tommy got them back to the library.*

There was one framed photo of a woman and two boys. The twins couldn't have been more than ten in the photo. The woman was smiling and the boys were obviously standing still against their will and seemed to be rolling their eyes but neither looked unhappy. In the corner stood a yoga mat rolled up with a yoga brick next to it. Based on the number of books he had he probably could have taught our class better than my cousin. There was a poster of Van Gogh's sunflowers on the wall but otherwise the walls were bare.

The kitchen had a toaster oven and tea kettle on the counter but not much else. There were no dirty dishes, no dirty coffee cup on the counter, nothing to show someone was living here two days ago. As I turned to the dining room, I saw there were painting supplies and an easel taking up the bulk of the space where anyone else would have had a dining set. One thing that was odd, or at least unexpected, was that there were flowers everywhere. Little vases and glasses dotted every table or counter filled with wildflowers you would find in the town park. They were probably fresh a couple of days ago but they were starting to die. I wasn't sure if I would be allowed to throw them out before they became sadder, so I left them. I know Tommy said the police were done with the apartment, but I wasn't sure the next of kin would appreciate me touching anything. Actually, I probably shouldn't be here as it was.

I went through the bedroom door and the theme of simple continued. The bed was just a mattress and box spring neatly made with a plain blue duvet. There was a nightstand and a dresser, again with flowers decorating the top, but nothing else. The closet with sliding doors was on the right and a bathroom door opened on the left. Everything was neat and tidy but simple. He obviously wasn't spending money on decor. I backed out since I felt like I was intruding and went over to the canvases leaning against the dining room wall. I found the one Tommy had commissioned. Although he described it in detail, it helped Rodney had attached a Post-It note with "Tommy" written on it to the back of the picture. It was a beautiful painting of their cabin done from what appeared to be the opposite side of the lake. Rodney really was talented.

I picked it up and started to leave when Rodney's calendar caught my eye. He had the wedding date circled in red with "gig at resort" written on it and what appeared to be his work shifts noted on the bottom of just about every day. He also had "Darren" written on every other Wednesday at 10 a.m. Darren Mosley? Gwen's husband? My stylist's husband had a standing appointment with Rodney? I could ask her later since my appointment for a cut and style was today. He also had "Bro" and a time noted every couple of weeks. Other than that, his schedule seemed pretty empty.

As I went to lock the door back up I gave the apartment one more look. It took the concept of minimalist to a new level. There were no signs of modern technology other than the stereo and tea kettle. And those were hardly modern by today's standards. Just a few personal items or photos chronicling his life. It was kind of sad. If I didn't know better, I would say it reminded me of a monk's cell.

~~~

I made it to Tommy's cabin in good time. It was after rush hour and before any kind of lunch rush. I pulled up, grabbed the painting from the backseat, and walked up the front steps to the porch intending on leaving the painting on one of the Adirondack chairs when the front door opened and Mateo, in all his glory, walked out.

"Maddy … sweetie, you didn't knock," he accused. He made this cute sad face that I knew I wouldn't be able to walk away from. Mateo was the definition of tall and lanky. Although he and I were the same height, his thin frame always made me think he was taller. He had dark almost black hair buzzed on the sides and longer on top. It was always falling in his eyes, which were this clear shade of green that were absolutely stunning. He still had the coloring of his Spanish heritage but there was no sign of his accent. His parents had immigrated from Cuba when he was a baby, so he only fell into the dialect when his mother was around or he got worked up about something.

"I didn't want to disturb you guys. Happy Anniversary," I cheered as I walked over to give Mateo a hug. He was a hugger. And he gave good hugs. Somehow, hugs are less annoying when they are coming from good huggers. Tommy walked out and joined us and I gave him a "what did you want me to do" look. He just nodded but I still felt bad about intruding. You couldn't be mad at a cat for being a cat and you couldn't be mad at Mateo for being Mateo.

"Of course, you can disturb us. Besides, we were just taking a slow morning. I just made tea. I still have hot water. You'll have a cup, and we'll catch up. I want to make sure you are okay after your trauma," Mateo said, and he was off before I could decline or even agree. With Mateo you just kind of held on and let nature take its course.

"I'm sorry," I apologized to Tommy. I knew he didn't take a lot of time off, so I felt really bad about intruding.

"It's fine. He's right, we were just taking a quiet morning. We aren't on any kind of schedule. And now maybe you can answer his questions, so I don't have to try to remember what you told me. He's never known anyone who found a dead body." He rolled his eyes while explaining. "So, you are a big topic of conversation right now anyway." Mateo had an insatiable curiosity so it was to be expected he would want to know every detail. He would have made a great cop.

"So, tell me, was it gruesome?" Mateo asked, cutting right to the chase. He handed me a mug of tea just the way I liked it and we took seats on the Adirondack chairs that decorated their front porch. I had to admit I loved their cabin. It was set back from the lake on a small hill but with a stunning view. It didn't have water access, which was probably the only reason Tommy could afford it when they bought it ten years ago. It was a simple two-bedroom layout. One large room was the kitchen, dining, and living room and then there were two bedrooms that shared the one bath. It did have a fireplace, which dominated one wall, and photos of friends and families covered the other walls. Mateo had added color by decorating all the rooms with bright pillows and blankets, contrasting nicely with the natural wood.

"No. He was just lying there. I didn't know a person could be that still honestly," I confessed. I hadn't thought about it until right then. How still he was. To see a body totally devoid of life was truly a different, and probably life altering, experience. A chill suddenly ran up my spine and I shivered.

"Oh, Maddy, I'm so sorry. We don't have to talk about it," Mateo apologized and reached out to hold my hand. I could tell he felt bad now and it wasn't really his fault. He had a huge heart and I know he genuinely regretted asking.

"It's okay. I guess I just didn't realize how it affected me until now. And I feel bad because I didn't look for him when he didn't show for the wedding," I confessed. And I did. To know he had been back there for the entire event. I just felt badly for Rodney.

"I am also realizing I didn't know that much about him, other than

53

basics."

"Well, I can help with that," Mateo said, suddenly cheering up.

"How so?" I asked. I didn't realize Mateo knew him as more than Tommy's bartender.

"We both volunteered at the same animal shelter," Mateo said. "He and I were there the same two days a week and spent time talking while walking dogs and playing with the cats." I knew Mateo volunteered at the Lake Wilson Animal Shelter. He had hit me up for enough donations and fundraising contributions over the years. He loved all animals and Tommy had cut him off at home after three cats. Larry, Curly, and Moe were so adorable even Tommy couldn't say no when Mateo brought them home.

"What was he like?" I asked as I took another sip of tea and got comfortable. I knew from experience Mateo was going to share everything he knew about Rodney.

"Well," he began as he also got comfortable, "he is Roger Atkins' younger brother. Even though they are twins, Roger was born first. And Roger never let him forget it. You know Roger, the bank manager at LW Savings and Loan?" I nodded, not wanting to interrupt. "Rod got out of prison right before he came back. He served eight years for fraud or something. He called it a stupid mistake when he was a senior in college. Apparently, he got in over his head when he was trying to cut corners while making tuition money. I'm not sure about all the details. He didn't talk about the fraud itself. The one good thing was he saw prison as the place where he found his true purpose. He started reading a lot about Buddhism in prison when one of his cellmates introduced him to yoga. Anyway, it was life changing so he threw himself into it. The whole, not stepping on ants thing and all. He donated about half his pay to the animal shelter to make up for his 'mistakes as a former carnivore' as he called it."

"Then why work at The Dive?" I asked, honestly curious. "I mean, they serve burgers and chicken. Or is Tommy going vegan and just hasn't announced it yet."

Tommy spit out his coffee and made a mess, but luckily restricted it to his sweats. "Hell no," he answered more emphatically then necessary. We all laughed. Tommy was never known for passing up a burger on cheat day and wasn't about to start any time soon.

"He needed the job and it's hard to get one with a record like his," Mateo explained. "He was saving up. He wanted to get off parole and go to

Tibet or somewhere like that. I don't think he had many more interests than that. His life seemed to be work, the animals, and his studies. He didn't even drive. I was actually surprised he got the wedding gig. I didn't realize you and Jess knew him."

"We didn't know him well. At least, we didn't know he had DJing experience," I admitted. "Carl asked us to hire him. It was literally the only thing he requested at the whole wedding. He didn't even care about his groom's cake. We couldn't turn him down. And when Jess had talked to Rodney, she said he knew what he was doing, had some experience, and that was enough for me."

"Wait, Carl asked for Rodney? A cop hiring an ex con isn't something you hear about everyday" Tommy asked. Now that he put it that way, it did sound a bit odd.

"Yes. Carl is another volunteer at the animal shelter. He's more of a dog guy, but none of us are speciesists. We all talk to each other while volunteering. I know Carl wanted to invite some of the staff to the wedding, but I guess the Bartons put a limit on the list," Mateo explained. That was news to me, but I let it slide.

"Yeah, he said he DJed during college. I guess that is where he got his bar experience. I just don't think he socialized much once he got out. I wonder if there will be a service? I would want to pay my respects." Mateo looked at Tommy for an answer.

"No clue. Roger didn't mention it when I told him he could take his time cleaning out the apartment if he needed it. He actually said I could throw it all out. He didn't seem interested in Rod's stuff," Tommy said.

"But all the art?" I asked. I just couldn't believe his brother wouldn't want at least one or two of the paintings. They were really very good. "And there are library books so make sure you return them."

Tommy nodded. I was pretty sure I was going to have to remind him a few times.

"Well, let me box it up and keep his stuff in the storage unit for a while. Roger might change his mind. If he doesn't, we can at least hang some of his paintings at the shelter. Maybe make a tribute of it?" Mateo decided.

"Speaking of his art," Tommy hinted while looking at me. I got the hint and got up, thanking Mateo for the tea, and took my leave. I knew Tommy wasn't big on PDAs and giving Mateo his gift was going to qualify so I headed for my car and refrained from turning around when I heard Mateo's squeals of joy. I was happy for my friends.

~~~

If left to my own devices I would probably walk around with my hair in a ponytail every day for the rest of my life. However, I am rarely left to my own devices. So, when I moved back home, I started going to A Cut Above to tame my notoriously uncooperative hair. Gwen Mosley opened A Cut Above when she and her husband John moved back here from the city about ten years ago. She had graduated a couple of years behind me and then moved to work in one of those trendy salons for a while where all the employees have to wear black, and they serve you mimosas. I guess all those years of black and stainless steel took their toll and Gwen's place was probably the classiest tribute to country living you were going to find. She even had Luke Bryan playing most days.

When I walked in this morning, "Country Girl" was playing and Gwen was finishing up with a client. I waved to Gwen and she let me know she would be with me in five. The salon was painted a warm gray with the wall divided by white plank wainscoting. There were six stations spaced out generously and each was personalized by the stylist who used it. Jess's sister Monica had the station on the opposite side of Gwen and had just started working on someone's highlights. They were deep in conversation about the latest *Grey's Anatomy* episode.

Gwen finished up with her client and asked me to head on back to the shampoo chair. I swear, if you could give a Noble Prize for scalp messages Gwen would be a shoe-in. It was the five minutes of pure bliss I was guaranteed every eight weeks. I imagine it was the same sensation cats felt when they started to purr. I assumed the position and reclined in the chair.

"Hey, girl, I hear you had an interesting weekend," Gwen said as she turned the water on and tested for temp. As she began to wash my hair, I realized she was probably one of the first to know what happened. Her salon was Grand Central Station for gossip and she probably knew Rodney was dead before I did. Also, her husband Darren was a parole officer and more importantly, based on his calendar, Rodney's parole officer. Besides, it had been almost forty-eight hours so I was sure she had more information then Nick or Scott could dream of. They probably should have questioned her even though she wasn't at the wedding.

But then I remembered she and a few of her staff were hired to handle the hair and makeup for the bridal party that morning so she had spent most of the day at the resort. All the women in the party had gathered in a suite for the preparations before the wedding. Gwen was probably working non-stop for hours before the actual event.

"Yeah, it was certainly a shock," I answered when she finished up with my wash. I really needed to stop in more often. It just felt so good. "How's Darren handling it? Rod was one of his clients, right?" I asked innocently.

"He was. And he was probably as shocked as you. Rod was really walking the straight and narrow. Just between you and me, Darren said he was one of the few clients he had that he was convinced would make it. He had really put his past behind him," she said.

"I'm not even sure exactly what he did, but he did seem to be all about peace and caring. I didn't know he had been volunteering at the animal shelter," I added.

"Three days a week or something like that. I really think he just got in over his head as a kid. He ran some kind of mail fraud. He got a copy of the college's letterhead and started sending delinquency notices to parents. Saying their kids owed money on their food account or something. He put a P.O. Box on it and the parents thought it was legit. They sent in thousands. When he got busted, he said it was all him. No one believed him but he refused to give his partners up, so they sent him up for a while based on the amount of money he got away with," she explained, filling in the blanks leftover from Mateo.

"Wow. He didn't strike me as the type who could master mind something like that," I confessed. It's not that Rodney struck me as stupid. But there is a big jump from not stupid to criminal mastermind. He seemed more like pawn material to me.

"Yeah, Darren thought he had a real chance at turning his life around. And he doesn't feel that way about all his clients," she added. I don't know that it made Rodney's death more tragic, but it did strike me as a little sad. But enough gloom and doom. Gwen was one of the few people who might know where people were right before the wedding.

"All the girls looked great at the wedding. You did a phenomenal job," I complimented. Gwen did Stacy, Lucy, and a bridesmaid or two. Monica and another stylist did the rest of the wedding party including Carl's mom. They got to the resort at 6 a.m. to set up in the suite we had reserved for preparation. We had a small breakfast buffet set up and mimosas were served for the wedding party while the women waited their turns. We were smart enough to stop the champagne around 11 so no one would be drunk at the ceremony.

"Thanks. I'm not going to lie, I was worried when I took the job because Lucy can be so ... particular," Gwen confessed. "But we had done so much to change her color and style in the couple months before that it wasn't hard at all. And given how everyone was in and out all morning, it was a good thing because we were running short on time by the time she got her turn in the chair."

"That's a lot of commitment to one event," I said amazed. "I mean, I know your daughter's wedding is important but months of appointments to change your hair? That is serious devotion."

"No, it wasn't just for the wedding. She's overhauling her whole look. She's got some kind of idea in her head how she is entering a new phase of her life and what someone of her 'standing' as a member of the community should look like and she's putting it in to full effect," Gwen explained. "I guess with Stacy married she'll have free time to do more in the community. A lot of empty nesters do it, the new look thing. But she is taking it to a new level."

"That's odd. I mean, Stacy is a grown adult with a job. It's not like she took up Lucy's time with afterschool running around or something. But maybe she was more invested in Stacy getting married than I thought. And now that you mention it, she has looked more put together than before. Reggie's business must be booming between the wedding and her new outlook."

"Not sure about that, but Lucy is spending like she's got a money tree in the backyard. And she has all these plans for her future. She's really embracing the empty nester stage of life. More power to her, I guess." Gwen sounded as confused as I was with the whole subject. Gwen never was impressed with things like that. She was a big believer that a dye job and made-up face didn't mean you were a better person.

My cut took its usual thirty minutes. I found a style that worked and stuck with it. Gwen wouldn't let me do anything that looked bad, so I stopped recommending shaving it all off a while ago. When I first separated, I tried to convince her it was a symbolism of my clean start. She said extreme changes may be a sign of a new start, but that didn't make them a good idea. Just because you can doesn't mean you should, as my mom used to say.

As I finished up, the bell on the door chimed and as usual, we all turned to see the new arrival. It was Sarah Stevens, the suspected owner of the mystery bracelet. I was debating whether to mention it to her. If it wasn't hers then why should she care, and if it was, then the cops would tell her about it. I mean, how do you start that topic? "Hey, I found your bracelet next to a dead body." Yeah, they really needed a handbook for this stuff.

I was paying and making my next appointment with the receptionist when Sarah solved the dilemma for me.

"Hi, Maddy. I wanted to thank you for finding my bracelet," she greeted me. "But, I'm just wondering … are you sure you found it at the wedding?" I had to admit I hadn't really had any interaction with Sarah before the wedding, but I imagined this is how she asked little Tommy if he ate the last cookie. Sarah was an elementary school teacher at Lake Wilson Elementary and was born and raised here. She only left town to go to college at State. She was really a very attractive girl with long chestnut brown hair and lovely brown eyes that stood out even without makeup. And she had a shape like a 50s pin up. She was engaged to a local real estate agent and they made a striking couple. The kind who you wondered how good looking their kids would be.

"Hey, Sarah. Yes, I found it when I went to look for my bag. Why?" I asked. This was not something I was likely to forget. I realized I felt somewhat guilty even though I didn't actually do anything wrong by turning her bracelet in. In fact, Nick might tell you I didn't do it soon enough.

"I lost it a couple of days before and I've never been in that closet so I just don't know how it could have been found there," she explained. "And I certainly wouldn't have been there with *him*," she added strongly. Well now, that was not what I was expecting. I mean, I didn't even know she knew Rodney let alone held him in such low regard. But how else would it get there? Unless she just didn't want anyone to know she had been there.

"Well, where did you think you had lost it?" I pushed. "I mean, if you know where you didn't lose something maybe you have an idea of where you did." Besides, she started this, so I wasn't being nosy, I was helping to hold up my end of the conversation. Yup … that's it. I was only being polite. Dear Abby would be proud.

"See, that is what is so odd. The last time I remember seeing it was at Lucy's when we were working on the wedding favors. We were tying the candy boxes with the embossed ribbons and I noticed it missing on my way home. I checked my car inside out and didn't find it so I figured I would ask Stacy, I just didn't get around to it," she elaborated. She was tapping her fingers on the desk and really seemed to be giving the issue thought.

"So, who was there that night?" I asked, thinking maybe there would be some logical explanation for the whole thing in the guest list.

"Just the wedding party, us girls. Kind of a last hurrah and all," she offered. Well, that was no good. None of the wedding party had a reason to be in the closet so that didn't really help.

"Well, maybe one of them found it and dropped it?" I offered. Even I knew that didn't make sense. But I just couldn't see Sarah doing anything nefarious. Although, this was also the first time I had heard anyone say anything remotely negative about Rodney.

Before we could keep speculating, Gwen called her and she walked to the back of the salon. Well, now I was confused. And I didn't like being confused. I was going to have to do something about that.

Chapter Eleven

As I was getting into my car, I received a text from Jess that Jean-Paul could meet me at The Last Drop any time after 3 p.m. He would be working from there on meal planning for some dinner party he had this weekend. I had noticed that his contact information Jess had forwarded didn't have a street address, just a phone number and email. I guess it could be explained that he hadn't been in town long, just six months, so he hadn't found time to rent an office space. Nevertheless, I found it odd.

I noticed Jean-Paul as soon as I walked into The Last Drop. I waved to my cousin, Crispin, as I walked toward his table. Crispin was my cousin on my mom's side. Her side of the family, the Beale's, were a little more unconventional compared to my dad's side. One rather odd feature was that all my uncles and aunts married someone with the same initials and named their children with that same initial. So, Crispin came from the C's. His parents were Cleo and Chris and his siblings were Cat and Charlie. It did make it easier come family tree time.

He had opened The Last Drop after working in the Peace Corp. He returned home, married, and decided he needed to find an outlet for his creativity, but one that made money. He was one of those coffee aficionados who smelled beans, roasted his own, and made all kinds of special blends. It was all lost on me. I was one of those rare people who couldn't stand the stuff.

Jean-Paul was busy typing away on his laptop and didn't notice me until I made it to the table. It gave me time to observe him. Since I worked in conjunction with The Resort on the wedding, I didn't have to have a lot of the vendor contact I normally would for an event. Jess handled the food since it would be The Resort's kitchen that served the reception. I had assumed we would use their chef until Lucy informed us at one of our meetings that she had found a fabulous "up and coming" chef in the area and she had been lucky enough to book him. I'll admit red flags were going off left and right and normally I would have tried to talk a client out of such an untested chef. However, there was no way Lucy was going to risk ruining the high point of her social career on a so-so meal, so we let her make the call. It didn't stop me from putting it in about three emails that we were using "her handpicked caterer" and not the one The Resort offered. There was no way I wasn't covering my ass on that one.

As I approached his temporary office, I noticed he was dressed smartly. His black work pants were ironed with a crisp crease and he had a maroon chef's jacket on with his name embroidered on the right pocket. He even had polished black shoes, but they were clearly made for standing long hours. His almost pitch black hair was slicked back and he was clean-shaven. At the reception I noticed his eyes were always wary of who he was talking to, almost as if he measured you up already and found you lacking. But Jess said he had never been anything but professional and his food really was outstanding.

"Hi, Jean-Paul, I hope this is a good time. Jess said she had reached out to you," I greeted him. I never knew when to interrupt people when they were obviously working. I mean, what if they never take a natural break? Standing here waiting would get awkward quickly. Just as I was getting ready to sit down, Crispin came over with my tea. One of the advantages of your favorite cousin running the local coffee shop is his knowledge of your intense hatred for the stuff. He kept my favorite tea in stock for my regular visits. If you didn't know better you would think I was a coffee addict based on how much time I spent here.

"Yes, she mentioned you might need my assistance," he answered. He was appraising me again and I felt even more lacking than normal. I wondered where he learned how to do that. It was a great skill if you had it but being on the receiving end stunk. I opened my tablet and pulled up the event I wanted to discuss with him.

"I have a birthday party I am arranging for a client and they have requested a Middle Eastern feast. The inspiration for the theme is *Scheherazade's 1001 Nights*. It's not for almost two months, but I was hoping you would be willing to tackle the challenge," I said encouragingly. I was trying to cater (haha) to his ego. He had struck me as someone who enjoyed showing off their talents.

"Hmmm … so unique for this quaint town. Somewhat surprising that a Lake Wilson resident would want something so exotic and flavorful." His interest was obviously sparked. I guess he thought we would all be asking for meatloaf and mashed potatoes? But given his clientele so far had consisted of mostly Lake Wilson's elite vacation homeowners, I would have thought boredom hadn't set in yet. When Lucy hired him, she mentioned he had been doing high-end dinner parties for some of the vacationers and developers temporarily living at the lake during the beginning of the project.

"Yes, well, you only turn seventy-five once. The family is renting out one of the lake houses for the event and wanted to do a buffet set up. There will be about eighty people for the party and they were requesting two hors d'oeuvres tables in different rooms to limit crowding and then the main meal set up in the great room. I know they had not settled on dessert yet, but wanted at least one dessert station and possibly two if they end up not getting a cake. There will be seating inside and out," I laid out for him.

"And who will be providing the bar?" he asked. He had started taking notes and I appreciated his total attention. I hated when vendors only half-listened and then came back with questions we had already covered. One brownie point for him.

"That is being taken care of. Apparently one of the grandchildren runs a bar a couple of towns over and is even working on a signature cocktail. Normally I would ask you to handle that as well but this is a unique situation," I explained. If we were going to be working together in the future, it would only be fair to let him know what I would normally expect.

"Also, the serving staff would have to be wearing costumes. The client will be covering the cost of the rentals of course, but I thought I would let you know now," I tried to sneak in.

"Costumes?" he said disapprovingly. I mean really, he was all but grimacing. And honestly, I'm not sure I could blame him. A birthday party did not normally call for staff to do anything more than serve. This wasn't a Renaissance festival or anything after all.

"Yes, they are looking for complete immersion in the evening," I said, wanting him to know it was not my idea. Although I respected the commitment. They were even planning on decorating the house to theme. I just hoped throw pillows didn't result in people tripping everywhere. Broken hips had a way of ruining a party.

"Of course they are," he said while rolling his eyes. "I can put together a menu and a quote for you by tomorrow. I want to address any issues fairly quickly. I don't like leaving things until the last moment. I do have a dinner party this Friday for some very important bankers and it must have my attention, but I should still be able to get the first draft to you," he explained. The way he made it sound you would think it was open-heart surgery instead of grilled salmon, but better a passionate chef than a boring one, I guess.

"That will be fine. We have some time. Jess mentioned you'll bring in a crew and just need access to the kitchen the day before. Is that right?" I asked. This was an odd request but since he didn't have office space yet I figured he didn't have a proper catering kitchen yet, too.

"That is correct. I have not found a suitable facility which to buy yet," he informed me. I knew if he wanted something in town, he would have to design it from the ground up. We didn't have anything close to a professional kitchen sitting around waiting for someone to snatch it up.

I decided now was as good a time as any to get to know our new resident gourmet better. And maybe figure out how he and Rodney knew each other, or at least why they argued.

"That shouldn't be a problem. And I'll let you know if I hear of any properties that might work. Jess mentioned you went to the C.I.A. Albany is such a walkable city don't you agree," I asked. Going to such a prestigious school would explain part of his ego but certainly not all of it.

"Yes, it is. Small for a city and the palate is so boring once you leave campus. But staying stateside it was really the only choice," he finished. He started working on his computer again signaling my dismissal. He really should have taught in a Catholic school or something. He had the air of superiority down pat. He wasn't getting rid of me that easily.

"Well, there was certainly more excitement at the Barton wedding then you would normally find," I baited. His face broke its cold disinterested facade for just a second but he quickly recovered. If Nick could drag Jess to the suspect list based on one venting session then a full-blown argument should shoot Jean-Paul straight to the top.

"Ah yes, I heard you had found the victim. I do hope it wasn't too traumatic for you. I wasn't familiar with the gentleman, but I heard he was supposed to be working the wedding in some capacity," he stonewalled.

"He was. He was hired to be the DJ actually. And that's odd, someone had mentioned they saw you and Rod in a rather heated discussion before the reception," I explained, being deliberately vague. I didn't want him to get too defensive. Besides, he didn't strike me as the type who was going to enjoy being called out.

"He was just in my way when we were preparing, nothing more serious than that," he explained dismissively. There's no way Jess mistook a heated discussion for two people passing in a close hallway. He was lying, and that just made me wonder what they really discussed. But he had effectively ended the discussion.

I got up, returned my cup to Crispin and paid for my tea. He always refused my money so I just put a couple bucks in the tip jar. I was feeling particularly generous. After all, it looked like I had a caterer for an unusual party and I knew the town's new arrival much better. I even knew he never attended the Culinary Institute of America, which was not located in Albany. Very productive indeed.

~~~

Tommy sent me a text just as I was walking through my front door.

T: Need you to cover for Rod tonight. Haven't found anyone to replace him yet and there's hockey and basketball tonite. Start at 6?

M: There better be potato skins included with pay.

T: Of course. And don't forget your Dive shirt. Would hate to have to write you up. ;) Thanx

That gave me just over an hour to get ready. I was beginning to regret taking the bartending class in college, but it was a great way for an introvert to learn social skills and to make a few bucks while not having to work retail. When Mitch's career started to take off it made me very popular at dinner parties. Guests would try to stump me with requests. It got to the point I would study up on the newest drinks. When Tommy realized I still knew how to mix a drink and draw a pint he started asking me to cover for him when he was shorthanded. In some perverse way, I still loved it and working at The Dive was the best of both worlds. I knew ninety percent of the patrons and got to pour drinks. It also kept me in the loop on town news. Drunk men around a bar were better than a hair salon any day of the week for finding out the latest gossip. But I was worried I would be the center of attention tonight, not the patrons.

While I was relaxing in a bubble bath (see ... good place for a playlist) I realized that I knew a lot more about Rodney's murder today then I did yesterday but all it had done was raise questions. What could Rodney and Jean-Paul possibly be arguing about? How could Sarah's bracelet end up in that hallway? And why would anyone possibly want to kill a yoga practicing, cat loving painter/bartender? This really was just getting more mysterious the more I learned. Maybe tonight would give me the chance to work some of it out in my head. At the very least, I could drown my frustrations in plastic cheese.

I put on my comfortable bartending shoes and headed out of the house with time to spare. I wasn't planning on drinking, but I still decided to walk since spring was in full effect and it was supposed to be a clear night. As I walked down my front path, I realized Mateo was scheduled to come over this weekend and tame the craziness that was my front garden. Not only did I not have a green thumb, I had the thumbs of black death. I couldn't keep a flower or plant alive to save my life, so Mateo was totally responsible for keeping Aunt Aggie's garden in the pristine condition it found itself.

As I entered The Dive fifteen minutes later, I saw that Tommy's assistant manager, Brian, was working the bar and he waved me over. He was clearly being pulled in a hundred directions and was relieved to see me.

"Reinforcements!" he celebrated. "We had a server and a dishwasher call out so I need to be working the floor and the kitchen if you think you can handle the bar yourself?" He looked hopefully at me. I know he didn't want to call Tommy any more than I did since it was his anniversary. Besides, it was locals tonight so they could wait a minute if needed. No one was in a rush with both the Penguins and Flyers hockey games on.

"No problem," I said. It was mostly going to be draft bears and the occasional bourbon so I was pretty sure I could keep up. I got behind the bar and started taking orders. The night was going pretty smoothly, and the Penguins were losing so it was a good night to be at The Dive. I was relaxing and catching up with regulars when about halfway through the third period Roger Atkins walked in and took a seat at the bar. I don't know if I ever recall seeing him here before. I know Tommy mentioned he fought with his brother a few nights ago, but this wasn't Roger's kind of place. He was more of a wine bar customer. Or even the country club scene.

"What can I get you?" I asked him, placing a napkin in front of him.

"What are you doing here?" he asked incredulously. I had to bite my tongue about not serving that particular drink and decided it was a chance I wouldn't normally have since Roger and I didn't run in the same social circles. His chinos and button-down shirt didn't fit with either the hockey or basketball crowd.

"I'm covering for Tommy. It would normally have been your brother's shift and they needed someone," I explained. I felt as if I almost had to remind him his brother had just died and had a life.

"Oh, yes. Very sad. I was actually here to talk to Thomas and see about getting the key to Roger's apartment. I need to clean out his belongings and any paperwork he might have. I am his sole beneficiary after all," he replied. Now, I didn't know Rodney's personal financial situation well and I did have the unfair advantage of having visited his apartment today but even I knew there wasn't going to be any "paperwork" among his possessions. Also, no one ever called Tommy Thomas.

"Well, Tommy will be back tomorrow. He is not here tonight. I'm sure if you call him in the morning, he can meet you at Rod's apartment," I offered. There was no way I was letting him know I had been there this morning. He probably would have demanded an accounting of what I had done and I didn't think Roger was owed that.

"That will work. I should be able to fit him in. And I'll have the opportunity to talk to him about the new vacation development coming to Lake Wilson. It might be something Thomas would be interested in investing in. I know he's done a lot of real estate investment in town but really the trend is moving toward the lake. And with the area on the north side now being developed it opens all new opportunities. They resolved all that ridiculous protracted litigation so now the full potential of Lake Wilson can be realized," he said. I wholly expected for him to whip out an American flag as he finished. I'm not sure what the full potential of Lake Wilson was and I wasn't sure I wanted to know.

"I thought that was mostly out of town developers?" I asked cautiously. I didn't want to burst his bubble, but those developments almost never used our local banks for financing those types of property purchases. Sure, people might get their mortgage through the bank, but the big time out of town developers almost always came with their financing already figured out. And he clearly did not know Tommy if he thought he would invest in lake development.

"Well, they've realized the benefit of the personal touch our bank can offer. And we are working very closely with ALL the parties, so for a limited number of local investors with the right resources I could get them an introduction to the *right* people." He was beginning to sound more and more like a sleazy used car salesman. And I was beginning to see there really was nothing he and Rodney could have in common.

"Well, I think calling him tomorrow morning would be your best bet," I reiterated. "And I just wanted to let you know how sorry I was about your brother. You have my deepest condolences." I changed the subject. "I am an only child and often wished I had a sibling. I can't imagine how hard it is to lose one in such an unnatural way,'

"It is horrible. And now there's all the paperwork and follow up that has to be done," he said exasperated. Wow ... talk about shallow. I knew Roger was self-centered. Everyone in town knew that, but you would have thought he would draw the line somewhere. Whereas Rodney had been MIA for years, apparently serving time in the big house (*is that what it was called anymore?*), Roger had stayed local and tried to make a name for himself. He had been doing a pretty decent job of it, too. He had a solid job at the bank, was married, had two kids, and joined all the right community organizations. Then his wife found out that he had been fooling around with a number of her friends and she left him. Took the kids and moved back to her mother's in Boston. Apparently, if local gossip was to be believed, and it was usually reliable, she took him to the cleaners. Now he was seen as more of a lecher then a fine upstanding citizen.

"And even when you have differences with your brother so recently, I'm sure it is still so painful," I baited. What can I say? I wasn't going to let him get away with playing the victim. There was something about him that rubbed me the wrong way so I can't say I wasn't looking forward to making him uncomfortable.

"Differences?" he inquired.

"Yes, I had heard you two had a disagreement the other night right in this very bar," I answered.

"Oh, that. Just a philosophical difference. Nothing major. We just always saw the world differently. My brother didn't believe that power could be useful. He was always too altruistic," he explained rather vaguely. Now that

68

I could believe. But it still didn't explain what they had discussed.

"He never understood that ambition was not a bad thing. I mean, he was happy working here after all. He was never going to *be someone*," he scoffed. Did the man have any sense of social grace? Roger hadn't spoken more than ten words to me since my divorce. I fell off his radar when I was not longer married to a big-time corporate executive. But you would think he would refrain from insulting me to my face.

With that, Roger left The Dive. He could barely contain his superior smirk as he walked out. I was pretty sure he wouldn't have dared if Tommy were here. But Roger was one of those people who couldn't be bothered with you unless you had something he wanted … namely money.

The rest of the night was quiet, and I was first to go home since I was just filling in and would get in everyone's way when closing up. The night was a little cool so I was glad I had brought a light jacket. The walk home gave me time to wonder how two such different men could have been raised in the same family. I know people have different personalities, but their cores were so different. It was a puzzle … another one.

Chapter Twelve
Tuesday

The next morning I woke to an alarm. I'm not overly fond of them but they do serve a purpose. I had a 10 a.m. meeting with Mrs. Martell to plan the Lake Wilson Flower Society's annual Spring Fling. This was one of those events Aggie had always been in charge of, and I took over when I joined the business. This year's theme was "Busy as a Bee" and luckily the food was pretty simple so there would be no need to get too creative. The highlight of the event was the flower arrangement competition, and the members took care of that aspect. We were meeting at The Last Drop to go over some of the final arrangements.

I got ready and checked some emails while eating breakfast. Jean-Paul had sent me some menu ideas and asked some questions as to food allergies and preferences. He was thorough. And I was impressed he had put something together so quickly. No wonder Lucy recommended him. I noted that after Mrs. Martell's meeting I just had some emails to send but no other client meetings. I had kept the week pretty light to follow up on upcoming events before wedding season got heavy. The Spring Fling was the kick-off to the busy season. I had eight weddings this spring and summer, so I had a lot of work ahead of me.

I packed up my laptop and headed out to The Last Drop. I walked in about fifteen minutes before my meeting and Crispin waved me over to my normal table. It was off to the side of the cafe. Since the cafe was on a corner lot it still gave me prime people watching real estate. Crispin walked over with my Earl Grey and a blueberry muffin. He knew the way to a girl's heart.

"Hey there, Cuz," he greeted me warmly.

"Hey there. How's business?" I asked. Crispin was nearest to me in age and was probably the cousin I was closest to. He was laid back and didn't get too upset about things. The only time I had seen him lose his temper was when his wife Carrie was in a car accident and it turned out the driver had been drinking. I was pretty sure he would have killed the guy if left alone in a room with him. Carrie, or as my kids liked to call her, Cousin Tea Leaf, was the nicest person you would ever meet. And all she wanted was peace on earth and clean auras.

"Not bad. Turns out your cousin finding a body is good for business. You doing okay? I don't want to push but I just want to make sure you are okay," he responded. He was looking at me with concern. As annoying as having half the town being related to you could be it was nice to have so much support when things got weird.

"Honestly, it's disturbing. Finding him that way made it personal on some level. I just don't want someone to get away with having taken his life. From what I can tell, he didn't do anything to anyone. He kept to himself and just wanted to live a peaceful life. How could someone do that to him? Hell, I have more enemies than he does," I unloaded. I hadn't put it into words until now but there seemed to be a great injustice to me that someone did this. And to hit him from behind, when he was defenseless? It just angered me in a way I hadn't realized until now.

"Yeah, Carrie is pretty upset. She and Rod were friends. They had a lot in common," he said. Finally, something that made perfect sense. I could see Carrie and Rodney bonding over yoga, enlightenment, and all things chakra. It didn't occur to me until right now that she might be upset.

"Is she going to be okay?" I asked.

"Yeah, I'm making her take a couple of days off to grieve. She needs to find her center again. I may not be quite as into all of that as Carrie is, but I know she needs time." He loved Carrie so much you could hear it in his voice. She was a lucky woman.

Before we could continue, Mrs. Martell walked in and headed our way. Emily Martell had been the elementary school nurse for over forty years and upon retirement threw herself into beautifying our town with unparalleled devotion. She was exactly what you would expect of the president of the Lake Wilson Flower Society. She was wearing a flower pattern skirt and white blouse. She had sensible shoes on and carried a handbag that reminded me of Mary Poppins's carpetbag.

"Hello dears," she greeted. She took her seat and began to pull out her binder devoted to the Spring Fling. She had notes on every past event and plans for the upcoming ones. She was committed to not repeating themes or details. She refused to allow the society to become one of those stale organizations that simply threw the same party every year. She even made an attempt to follow the Rose Parade theme on a yearly basis for "continuity in the flower community" as she phrased it. Seeing as we were on the opposite side of the country, I think her devotion was lost on many but I appreciated it.

"Fine, Mrs. Martell, I'll get you your usual and let you ladies get to your business," Crispin said as he excused himself. He squeezed my shoulder as he passed. I used to be amazed at his memory until he told me he had note cards behind the counter listing everyone's favorite drinks and baked goods. While providing the coffees was pretty easy, Carrie didn't always bake the same items every day so that was more hit and miss. Although, how anyone could refuse a blueberry muffin was beyond me.

"So, child, have you recovered from your traumatic event?" she asked. Never one to beat around the bush, I expected nothing less. It was probably the reason why she was one of my favorite clients. I think it went back to her training as a nurse because she never struck me as rude, just direct.

"I'm fine, Mrs. Martell, it was unpleasant, but I am fully recovered," I fibbed. There was no reason to drag her into the matter. I knew that anything I told her would be all over town within a couple hours. While she was the picture of discretion when it came to patient health issues all else was fair game. Besides, we had a lot to cover today.

"It's just all so dreadful. And he was such a pleasant man," Mrs. Martell lamented. Wait … this was news to me. Mrs. Martell was not one for either The Dive or yoga so how did she know Rodney?

"Really, I didn't know you were friends?" I asked, legitimately curious.

"Oh, yes, we were good friends. He did his bendy exercises in the park near City Hall and I volunteer to help tend the gardens there. He said he loved to be surrounded by natural beauty when meditating. I admit, I thought he was a little flaky, but he was dedicated to his exercise and appreciated the hard work the Flower Society did to preserve those gardens. He would help weed and we talked for hours about the flowers. A few times, he even came to paint them. He gifted me one of his paintings. He was quite talented, a great addition to our town, unlike his brother," she answered. I was surprised with the distaste she displayed when mentioning Rodger. Mrs. Martell was not known for badmouthing others. She was more of the "if you can't say anything nice don't say anything at all" school of thought.

"Really? I know Rod was talented, but I didn't realize Roger had been so unpleasant," I prodded. I had a feeling Mrs. Martell would need very little encouragement.

"Oh, yes. He is probably the most unpleasant person I have ever encountered in this town. The society asks all the local businesses to sponsor our annual fundraising auction, the one held in November when we sell the poinsettias. You know the one, dear?" She looked at me for confirmation. Considering I also planned that one as my contribution, you would think she wouldn't need it.

"Yes, of course I do," I replied.

"You did such a lovely job last year with the banquet. It was my favorite so far," she sidetracked. "Anyway, back to Mr. Unpleasant. He said the bank would not contribute to keeping the town in the past. That flower societies were an outdated notion and were holding the town back from progressing. And to say this in front of Lucy Barton of all people. I mean, really, the nerve. I'm not stupid about progress but these are just flowers for goodness sake. What is wrong with wanting things to be pretty?" she asked.

"Nothing, the society does a wonderful job of making the town a prettier place to live." I figured a little flattery would go a long way.

"Exactly. He said once the new development was completed, we would not be needed and would have to find some other way to waste our time. He would make sure the town didn't waste resources on something so outdated. The nerve. I'm not sure who he thinks he is but lake vacationers have never dictated how this town is run. They don't consider themselves as full-time citizens and I don't know why that would change now. Besides, we don't take any money from the town. And he's not even a subcommittee chairman, let alone mayor," she finished. I could tell this had really shaken her.

"I'm sure he was just blustering," I assured her. "The society has been around for decades and it's not going anywhere now. He can't dictate how private citizens choose to spend their time."

"That's true. The town can't shut us down. I should have thrown that in his smug face. He just got my goat. But let's not waste any more time on the weasel. Maybe we could put a small memorial in the Spring Fling program to his brother. He would often help the members carry plants and supplies to and from their cars when we worked in the park. He was such a lovely boy," Mrs. Martell added.

"Of course we can," I replied. I made a note in the file. With that, we began our meeting. We covered quite a lot of issues and wrapped up a little after Noon. I stayed for another hour sending follow up emails and making sure the venue had our latest updates. One of the nice things about recurring clients is we knew how to get work done and didn't waste time getting to know each other.

I tipped Crispin, over his protests, and headed home to do some more work. As I was walking to my car, I spotted Sarah walking into the nail salon. I decided it would be a good time to confirm my appointment for next week so I headed across the street to Eva's Nail Palace and walked in while Sarah was just being added to the waiting list. I waived at Cousin Eva and was surprised when she called me over to her station. She had just finished up with someone and I figured Sarah was next.

"Maddy ... just in time for your appointment," Eva gushed way too excitedly. She got up and walked me over to one of the pedicure chairs. I knew my appointment was not today, so I was curious as to the Oscar worthy acting job.

"Oh good, I was worried I was late," I said, playing along. Eva, of the Beale side E's, started taking off my shoes and getting me situated in the massage chair. There were worse things in life than a spur of the moment mani/pedi.

"I am not working on that woman again," Eva whispered and then glared, yes glared, at Sarah. "She is beyond infuriating. I can handle pushy and rude but preachy is a whole other level with her," she explained. Eva was slightly judgmental of people, but usually not to a customer while they were there. Whatever Sarah had done must have been pretty bad since she was leaving her for one of her other nail techs. Eva never claimed to be perfect, in fact, she was pretty open about her moral failings, but that often made her fairly intolerant of those who thought they were above reproach.

"Hey, works for me," I replied. As I sat back, one of Eva's techs escorted Sarah to the chair next to me. I noticed she had a perfect French manicure on her toes and nails. Eva, as a rule, charged extra for French manicures because they bored her so much. I usually let her have her way with my nails since she knew my job and knew when not to go overboard.

"Any events the next two weeks I need to know about?" she asked. She was really good about making sure I didn't end up with a clashing color. Left to my own devices I would have had pale pink for life, but I had to admit I enjoyed the little flash of color more than I should have.

"I have the spring athletic dinner for the high school and that's about it," I answered. She went over and picked up blue and silver polish. They were our high school's colors so I figured she had an idea already.

"Oh, I didn't realize that was coming up," Sarah cut in. "We'll be attending as Neal is accepting an alumni award," she explained. I hadn't forgotten Sarah was engaged to Neal Bergstrom who was a local legend when it came to athletics. He was a poster child for a favorite son of the town. He went to college on a baseball scholarship and then came back to town to join his family's real estate agency. He and Sarah met in church and got engaged about six months ago. His mother was over the moon.

"Yes, it's next Thursday at the VFW hall," I added in case she forgot. Eva started working on my pedicure. Blue base coat, which inevitably meant I was getting some kind of silver bling. Polka dots were my bet since she now owed me, and she knows I love them. I'm not going to lie, my pedicures were the one area I tended to be a little daring.

"Oh, we'll be there. I should have asked you yesterday how you were recovering from your meeting with the police, but I was just so overwhelmed after talking to them myself. I imagine it was traumatic," she said almost excitedly. Was she hoping I was traumatized, or did she just want gossip?

"It was fine. Nick was very professional, and I was just confirming what I had already reported to them. I didn't see Rodney until I found him, so it's not like I had much to offer," I explained. I left it open hoping she would expand on her comments the other day.

"Oh, I would hope not. I briefly knew him in college, and he was not the type you would want to be associated with. It really was no surprise when he got in trouble back then, so it should be no surprise he came to such an end here," she said. That was pretty strong language coming from a Sunday school teacher.

"How did you know him in college?" I asked. Now I was curious. I got the impression yesterday she didn't really know him very well.

"We briefly worked together, but he was sketchy even then," she replied.

"I got the impression he had turned his life around recently," I defended. I don't know why I was so protective of him. I guess it always rubbed me the wrong way when people badmouthed those who were no longer around to defend themselves.

"A leopard never changes his spots. And that is a family of leopards. He was no better now than he was back then." She was bordering on fuming. With that, she opened her magazine and made a point of ignoring me. It gave Eva and me a chance to catch up. I continued to wonder what kind of interaction she had with Rodney that made her write him off as a lost cause.

When Eva was done with me, I had a brand new manicure proudly demonstrating my support for Lake Wilson high school athletics. I scheduled my follow up appointment and made my way home. It was still early enough so I should be able to get some work done today and Tommy hadn't asked me to cover again … yet.

As I got settled in my home office my text message chimed.

Jess: *Hey there, got a minute?*

Me: *Sure, what's up.*

J: *So, S and I had lunch. Turns out Roger turned in a cell phone he found at Rod's. Seems Rod was blackmailing some people.*

M: *jawdrop*

J: *Yup…you and me both. So far they only identified two but they know there was at least one more.*

M: *No cliffhangers…who*

J: *Sarah and JP. Not sure with what, just that he was leaving them drop off instructions and making threats.*

M: *What?!?! Neither of them is loaded so he wasn't going to get much. Are you sure?*

J: *Yup, I read over S's shoulder too so I made sure. Rog said he found phone in his brother's paintings when he cleaned it out. S is ticked the cops missed it.*

M: *Wait…in Rod's apt?*

J: *Yeah, why.*

M: *Just curious. But does make me wish I could talk to Sarah again.*

J: *You can if you can be here tomorrow at 11am. Her and her future MIL are checking out the ballroom as a possible wedding locale. It would be natural for you to be here for that.*

    M: *I'll be there. I'll even bring donuts. And why didn't you call?*

    J: *I'm in a staff meeting. Snooze.*

    M: *Pay attention...but first, is the Grill still serving that flank steak Cesar salad?*

    J: *Yup...why?*

    M: *Gonna invite JP for a biz lunch.*

    J: *oh you are sneaky. Ttyl*

    M: *:)*

Before I forgot I was being sneaky, I emailed Jean-Paul to invite him to lunch tomorrow to discuss his suggestions for the upcoming birthday party. I offered to treat … who can turn down free food? Especially at the Grill. And they really do have the best Cesar salad ever.

After getting his quick reply that he would be there at one I sat back in my comfy chair. I had to admit, Jess's news about Rodney being a blackmailer really threw me. No one had said anything bad about him other than Sarah. Now her comments certainly made more sense, but what made no sense was blackmailing an elementary school teacher and a just starting out caterer. Neither was loaded, at least not that anyone knew. And who was this third person? And how had I missed seeing a cell phone after looking through Rodney's paintings for Mateo's gift? And if you are blackmailing people how do you have nothing to show for it? Ugh … how is it that the more questions I asked the less I seemed to know about what was going on in my town?

Chapter Thirteen

Wednesday

The next morning I woke bright and early after my first good night's sleep since finding Rodney. I did a meditation and some yoga then got ready for my meeting at The Resort. Jess said to be there around 11 a.m. and I still had to pick a dozen donuts up at Slice of Heaven. I grabbed everything I would need to get some work done. If Sarah did decide to use The Resort I would most likely be helping Jess so I had to be prepared. Securing the gig wasn't my primary goal, but a job was a job.

When I walked into Slice the morning rush was over but Mrs. Carletti, Nick's mom, was refilling the donut trays for the mid-morning break customers. I asked for a dozen of her choice and threw in an apple muffin for the drive. What can I say, I don't share.

"Good morning, Madeline. How are you?" she greeted me. Mrs. Carletti was one of the only people who insisted on calling me by my full given name instead of the short form. She was in her usual uniform of khakis and a white shirt covered by a bright pink apron. Her dark brown hair was up in a bun and covered with a net. No one was going to find a stray hair in one of her pies. She had the same eyes as Nick but was short enough she barely managed to see over the counter.

"I'm good, Mrs. C, just here for donuts for Jess's staff," I explained. She knew all of us since Nick's house was on the regular rotation of home hangouts when we were kids. It helped that he was one of five so there were kids in elementary, middle, and high school to keep the house busy when I was growing up. You could pretty much show up at their house at any time to play.

"Then I'll make sure to include a raspberry donut for her." Mrs. Carletti knew everyone's favorite and I was going to get brownie points for showing up with one. It probably helped that Jess had been ordering the same thing since we were ten years old.

"Thanks. So, how is it having Nick back? Must be nice to have all your kids back in town?" I asked. As much as I would have loved to have both of mine here, they were at that point in their lives where they needed to explore and see the world.

"It's wonderful. Yours will come back, too. They just need to learn to appreciate home, it took Nick long enough." She blew a stray hair and rolled her eyes. "Now he just has to find a wife and I'll sleep better."

"Really? He needs one?" I asked surprised. I figured since she already had grandchildren the settling down pressure would have lessened.

"Yes, men who are married live longer. It's a fact," she informed me. I had heard that one, but I thought suggesting a healthier diet would be easier than finding a wife. But I was not going to argue with Mrs. Carletti. "Look at that moron stupid enough to let you go. He knew he needed one and married again."

I was lucky I wasn't drinking something, or I would have spit it all over my red blouse. I had to admit I didn't see that coming. My ex wasn't from this area so the town was decidedly pro Maddy when it came to talk of my divorce, but I had never heard it put so bluntly.

"I'm sure Nick will find someone when the time is right. Thanks for the donuts, Mrs. C," I said as I quickly made my safe getaway. I walked in thinking about work and Rodney's death and left with a muffin and a big smile on my face. Today might not be so bad after all.

When I walked out of the bakery I noticed a commotion down at the end of the street, There were a group of people standing around and I thought I heard sirens in the distance. I quickly walked down to the crowd, or what could be considered a crowd in Lake Wilson, and asked what was going on.

"It just came out of nowhere and hit him. He was just crossing the street," someone said.

I looked over their shoulder and there, in the crosswalk, was Roger Atkins. He was bleeding from a head wound and his left leg was laying at an odd and painful looking, angle.

"Did you see who it was?" I had no clue who asked.

"No, I was looking at him, but they didn't even stop to see if he was okay. I heard the hit and his screams. When I came out he was just lying there," another anonymous voice answered.

Just then, an ambulance pulled up near Roger. At some point, a patrol car must have arrived too because we were being pushed back to give the paramedics room to work. They quickly loaded him in the ambulance and took off. I hoped he would be okay. The officer was asking who, if anyone, saw anything. I had nothing to offer so I decided I should head out to The Resort where I might be able to talk to Sarah for a while. At least there, I might learn something.

~~~

I walked into Jess's office at 10:45 and handed over my care package. She immediately opened the box and pulled out her favorite before taking the rest out to her staff. I knew we didn't have much time before Sarah and her mother-in-law arrived so I let her enjoy her sugar rush in peace for five minutes. When she was wiping the last of the sugar off her fingers, I decided I could ask her about the new information.

"So, are we really sure the texts were blackmail? No other explanation?" I asked. I figured if I was going to bring it up with Sarah I had to at least pretend I knew what I was talking about. I was a big believer in fake it until you make it, but I had to have something to work with.

"Yes. I looked at the file and transcripts while Scott was in the bathroom—"*okay, TMI*—"and it is clear he made demands, was threatening to expose their secrets, and gave them instructions for drop offs," she explained. Gotta love a nosey best friend. But I guess she had a vested interest in this case.

"But I don't get it. Sarah doesn't have money. I mean, until she moved in with Neal she was sharing an apartment and her lifestyle is hardly extravagant. It's not like she comes from money. And how much do elementary school teachers make?" I really was confused. How much blood can you get from a stone exactly?

"I didn't even know Sarah and Rodney knew each other. I mean, Rod didn't run in her circles. Sarah teaches Sunday School and Rod is a Buddhist. I don't think I've ever seen Sarah at The Dive and Neal and Rodney weren't friends as far as I know," Jess said

"And how did Rodney know anything about Jean-Paul? I mean, Rod was from here and Jean-Paul is new to the area. And he doesn't seem to be loaded, either," I wondered aloud. Where was Aunt Aggie when you need her? "Oh, I can't believe I forgot to tell you. Roger Atkins was the victim of a hit and run this morning."

"You know, you lead with news like that, right?"

"Yeah, yeah, next time. But I was coming out of Slice of Heaven and he had been hit. Everyone was standing around. EMTs came and took him to the hospital."

"Is he okay?"

"I don't know. It just happened about an hour ago. It's not like the hospital is going to call me." I shrugged.

"You're telling me you don't have a cousin or something up there? That would be a first." She wasn't wrong. But truth was medical information was more than just idle gossip and there was no way I was risking anyone's job to find out how Roger Atkins was.

"Sarah and Mrs. Bergstrom are here." Jess plastered on her professional smile while waving at someone over my shoulder. Not gonna lie … it kind of scared me when she put on the professional face. I turned and saw them both being escorted to Jess's office by a member of the front desk staff. They looked surprisingly like mother and daughter dressed in their conservative knee-length pencil skirts and silk blouses with matching pearl-buttoned cardigans. I wonder if they got a bulk discount at Nordstrom's?

"Hello, ladies," Jess greeted them. This was her show, and I was more or less there in case there were questions about vendors that I was familiar with. Given how distracted I was about Rodney's murder it was probably good I was in a supporting role:

"Good morning, Jessica," Mrs. Bergstrom said as she entered. "I didn't know we would have company today?" she questioned while looking at me.

"Oh, Maddy is just here because sometimes we retain her to help oversee vendors and any details the bride and groom may request. She is strictly under our supervision," Jess explained. She was enjoying my newfound role as minion way too much.

"Of course. We don't anticipate needing an event planner. We are more than capable of planning the Neal's wedding. And after having helped

Lucy so much with Stacy and Carl's event we have a clear vision for the big day. It's only fitting that such well-established families celebrate in the town they have helped build. It is important this event represent Neal's position in the community," Mrs. Bergstrom explained in far greater detail then we were ever going to need. But her comment made me realize this was going to turn into a "whose wedding was better" contest between the two matriarchs. As far as I knew, this would be my first wedding where the groom was the focus instead of the bride. But as with Lucy Barton, I was pretty sure Mrs. Bergstrom saw this as her event rather than Sarah and Neal's.

I knew that Lucy's mom and Neal's mom both came from families that could research their families all the way back to the establishment of our town. But as much as I loved my home town that was hardly comparable to being on the Mayflower. Apparently, I had missed the importance to both ladies of their status. Maybe that is what happens when you spend fifteen years as a visitor rather than a resident. Lucy's family had been farmers and then business owners. Neal's family came from a long line of real estate agents. They had handled most of the home and commercial business property sales in the tri-county area for the last hundred years. I had bought and sold homes in the area and had to admit it didn't occur to me to call anyone else but the Bergstroms.

We continued our tour of the resort in general and then on to the wedding facilities. Jess gave a pretty thorough explanation of all the options available to the prospective bride and groom in creating their dream wedding. I noticed we avoided the back hallway. Although the whole area had been cleaned and re-carpeted, there was no need to tempt fate.

"Maddy, could you please show Sarah the bridal suite? Mrs. Bergstrom would like a better look at the garden and outside facilities," Jess interrupted my musings. She handed me the room key to one of the suites used by bridal parties to prep and Sarah and I made our way to the elevator.

"You must be so excited?" I asked Sarah as we entered the elevator.

"Oh, yes. I don't really care about the bells and whistles; I just want to be Neal's wife. And Mrs. Bergstrom has been great about the planning. I would be a bumbling mess, I'm sure. But it's important for a man in Neal's position to make the right impression. Have to make sure everyone who is anyone gets invited and all that," Sarah explained nervously. You could tell she had heard it often enough to repeat it verbatim. I honestly think she would have been just as happy going to city hall, at least that wouldn't lead to competing visions of taffeta in the coming months. I suddenly realized the younger generation of Lake Wilson residents was much more laid back then the older. But I guess that might be true all over.

As I opened the door to the fifth-floor suite, the nicest one Jess arranged for brides, I realized there would never be a better time for a totally awkward conversation than now. *Since awkward conversations were always awkward, did that mean that it was always a good time to have one?*

"I was just wondering one thing. Before you get married, are you going to tell Neal that Rodney was blackmailing you?" I asked rather indelicately. I know there were probably a dozen better ways to broach the topic, but they all failed me at the moment.

"Umm ... I don't have the faintest idea what you mean," she stuttered. I almost felt bad for making her so uncomfortable ... almost.

"The police know, Sarah. What I can't figure out is what Rodney could have had on you and what you could have possibly paid him?"

"Oh God, that's why they called this morning. I should have known he would haunt me even now." She began to cry.

"Sarah, tell me. Maybe I can help. Or at least be a shoulder," I told her. I wasn't big on hugging strangers, but I could put my arm around her and try to comfort her.

"It was all a stupid mistake. I was young and stupid and desperate," she started. "Remember when I mentioned Rodney and I worked together?"

I nodded, not wanting to interrupt her.

"It was in college. My family was trash and when I graduated high school, I ran and never looked back. But I was so desperate for money I didn't know what to do. I started waitressing and then dancing ... at a gentlemen's club. Rodney was the bartender and DJ at the bar. I didn't stay there long as I ended up getting a better scholarship. So, when I quit I never looked back. When he got out of jail and showed up here, I knew he would recognize me. But he didn't mention it and acted as if we had never met. I thought I was safe. It was about a month later I got the first text," she blurted out. I'm not sure she even took a breath.

"A text?" I asked. That just struck me as rather odd. I mean, I don't know much about blackmail etiquette, but I really thought texts were bad ideas. I mean, any married couple could tell you important conversations should never been done over text.

"Yes, said he would go to Neal and he had proof of my old job and that he needed me to help him," she continued.

"But what did you have that he wanted?" I finally got to ask. I realized under other circumstances that would sound insulting, but I could get away with it here.

"Information. He wanted to know what land the new developers were looking at up by the lake and how high they were willing to go. The new development is for the land behind the lakefront properties. They are being allowed to sell lake 'access' to docks and lake entries. He just wanted to know which areas they were looking at next. The lake is huge. It will take years before all the lots are built so he wanted to know what is next. A lot of the plots are owned but haven't been developed yet so Neal is helping the new builders to buy before the price is driven up. Kind of like Walt Disney in Orlando," she explained. That certainly made more sense than money.

"How did you get that kind of information?" I pushed her further. Might as well go for broke.

"Neal works from home a lot. I just looked over some of the paperwork. I sent him the plot locations and the limits they were willing to pay for each. But he said he had what he needed and stopped texting me a couple weeks ago. I thought it was over." She was struggling not to break down.

"Wait, you sent it to him ... how?" I followed up.

"By text ... it was all by text," she said, trying to control her hysteria.

"So you never confronted him? Talked to him about it?" I asked.

"No. We avoided each other. He acted like he didn't even know me when we saw each other. The only time we even talked in public was at the rehearsal dinner," she answered.

"When you spilled the wine," I finished for her.

"Yes, he had the nerve to ask me where I had gone to college. He was taunting me. It was so cruel," she confessed.

"So you didn't see Rodney the morning of the wedding?"

"No, I was busy with the hair and makeup people the whole time," she replied.

"Really? Because I heard that all of you were in and out all morning. So you could have snuck away and no one would have known where you went or really even how long you were gone," I pushed.

"I may have stepped out for a bit. Neal stopped by and needed to talk to me. So we found a quiet place for some private time." She was blushing. I mean bright red blushing.

"You mean you went off for a quickie?" I didn't mean to be indelicate,

84

but she wasn't getting that vague wouldn't work right now.

"Well, I don't know that I would use that word, but Neal wasn't used to me spending the night away and the bridal party had had a sleep over the night before so he just needed some quality time before the wedding."

Just as she finished, Jess and Mrs. Bergstrom entered the suite and were in the middle of discussing color schemes. Sarah turned and wiped any trace of potential tears away before they noticed.

"Well, how did the tour go? Any questions?" I covered for Sarah to give her a minute.

"It is a lovely facility. But we do have a few more places to tour before making our final decision," Mrs. Bergstrom replied. She was trying to give the impression to Jess that The Resort would have to compete for the event. But if she truly wanted a social event of any caliber there were few venues that could compete with The Resort. I figured Jess would get the call in about three weeks that they wanted to book for the wedding. Maybe next summer? There was a chance they would go for a winter theme, but I think she wanted to give Lucy a run for her money in spring weddings.

Jess escorted them out of the suite while I made sure we hadn't left any indication we were there. I followed behind while Jess gave her final pitch and it really was impressive. She played to both Mrs. Bergstrom's need for superiority over Lucy Barton and Sarah's dream of a fairy tale wedding to Neal.

I returned to Jess's office to kill some time before lunch with Jean-Paul. I didn't need to know the details or be there for any of the follow up questions. Resort business wasn't my concern until an event was booked and then only if Jess reached out. If they got the Bergstrom wedding then I would probably be needed, but until then I was a free agent. At least one mystery had been solved. Now I knew what Rodney was blackmailing Sarah with and what he wanted. It did seem a little out of character but if he really wanted to end up in Nepal or some such place, it wasn't going to be a cheap move. Especially if he wanted to keep giving half his pay to the animals. But what was he doing with the information?

~~~

I made my way to the Grill about ten minutes before my appointment with Jean-Paul. I had a better understanding of what the whole blackmail scheme was about now but needed him to explain his role in the big picture. If I managed to keep him as a caterer, all the better. I looked over the menu although I already knew what I wanted. The waitress brought me a Diet Coke right away. There was something to be said for being a regular.

Jean-Paul walked in precisely on time. I somehow got the impression he was always on time. As he got settled across from me, he ordered a sparkling water from the waitress. He was not a regular yet … sucked to be him.

"Thanks for meeting me here. I had a morning appointment, so I appreciate you agreeing to come," I greeted him.

"Not a problem. I am planning on seeing Jessica after to discuss an upcoming event so it works out well," he replied. I got the feeling he was ridiculously efficient in all things. We placed our orders and settled back to discuss business.

"Did you have a chance to review the initial menu and discuss it with the client?" he asked. He opened up his tablet and was prepared to take notes.

"I did. She was thrilled and is going to make a few notes. Not so much on any dietary restrictions but more along the line of favorites and preferences. I don't think it's anything that will change the authenticity." I was anticipating his objections.

"That's fine. I'm sure I can retain the authenticity of Morocco while making the client happy," he dismissed the concerns I had. I would have been upset but he really was a very good chef. I figured he was comfortable enough right now that I could try broaching the blackmail.

"I'm so sorry, by the way. I'm sure this must be a very distressing time, but I appreciate your professionalism," I explained. I was trying to be less direct for this discussion. I had a feeling he would close up if I just flat out asked.

"Distressing?" he asked with a raised eyebrow. I bet he waxed. No one got that kind of arch naturally.

"Yes, the whole *blackmail* thing," I dropped my little bombshell and my voice. Discretion never hurt. I was just relieved he wasn't drinking because he looked like he was going to choke. It was the first time I had seen his mask falter and on some level, it was kind of gratifying.

"I'm not sure I know what you are referring to," he tried to recover. Oh, hell no … he wasn't getting away with that.

"Yes, with Rodney blackmailing you. Now that the police know I'm sure they will be reaching out to you if they haven't already," I pushed. I had a feeling the only way I was going to get anything out of him was if he was uncomfortable.

"Shit … they know? How the hell did they find out?" He suddenly lost his polished tone and sounded more like he was from Hell's Kitchen. I had to admit I don't know that I was expecting that.

"Well, yes … they know. They found his phone. And while we both know you never went to the Culinary Institute, I'm pretty sure that is not what Rod had on you."

"It was the Albany thing, wasn't it? I realized after you left. That wasn't innocent small talk." He looked at me with a mix of respect and frustration. Here I thought I was being so secretive.

"No, but everyone pads their resume. What I don't get is what you could possibly provide Rod with. I mean, I don't think it was money … no disrespect," I pushed. "What information did he want from you?"

"It wasn't money. Every dime I make is going into the business. He wanted information on the developers. He wanted to know their big picture plan as he called it. He wanted to know how big the new vacation home project was going to be, what they were doing for financing, which properties they had already bought or bid on, and what areas were being developed in which phase, whether there would be commercial development, stuff like that," he admitted.

"How would you know that?" I asked. In all honesty, I had no clue how he would know anything about property development in a town he had not been in all that long.

"I cater for the execs when they come to town. While they ate, I took a look at the papers they had on their desk, sent the pics to Rod, and he agreed to shut his trap," he admitted.

"About what?" I followed up. I mean, seriously, resume padding wasn't that bad.

"We served time together at State. I thought I would be safe out here in the middle of nowhere. Then I walk into The Dive one night and he's behind the bar. What the hell are the chances? It was actually good to see him, and he played along with my new story so I thought he was going to be solid. Then I get a text that his silence has a price. Honestly, I didn't think he had it in him, but I guess he picked up a few things in prison," he explained.

"So how does a chef end up in state prison?" I had to admit to being curious. Things just didn't make sense yet.

"I wasn't a cook when I went in. I was a driver in an armed robbery. When I got in, they assigned me to kitchen duty. There was an old guy in there who had been a chef for a made man. He took me under his wing. Taught me all the skills of a trained chef. Then it was a matter of reading cookbooks and learning about different cultures. It passed the time. When I got out it seemed like the best way to go straight so I created Jean-Paul. So far, it has worked … until Rod. No one is going to allow an ex-con with access to their home. It's not so easy to get work when you leave prison."

"So what is your name?" I might as well go for broke. Our lunch arrived and we both thanked the waitress. Their Cesar salad really was the best thing ever. No reason not to eat while he answered.

"Mike Iancola. I didn't think it would sell as well for catering. But now it's all blowing up anyway." He really thought it was over.

"What was the fight really about then?" I figured I would push until he stopped. I took another bite. I had a feeling he was getting to the good part.

"I confronted him. I thought hiding behind texts was bullshit. He acted innocent and wanted to talk about it later. I guess getting in his face at a wedding wasn't the right time or place, but I was tired of it. He was pulling his 'changed man' crap and acting clueless. It honestly just pissed me off but we agreed to meet up after the wedding," he finished.

"Did you see him again at the wedding? After you confronted him?

"No, I was too busy in the kitchen."

"So, explain how it worked?"

"He would text me when I had an event telling me what he wanted and I would send it back to him later that night. Honestly, I think he was pretty much done with me. I had given him the whole project timeline and there wasn't much more I could tell him," he wrapped up.

"So, your argument didn't get more heated? Maybe moved to the hallway?" I asked

"What? No, of course not. Listen, I was ticked Rod pulled the blackmail card but it didn't warrant killing him. I've been to prison. I have no intention of going back. If I wanted him out of my life, all I had to do was move. It would have sucked, but I could have done it," he explained.

So, Jean-Paul/Mike provided the big picture, Sarah provided what the immediate steps were, and Rodney was using the information. But for what? I still felt there was one piece missing.

We both finished what was left of our lunch in silence. I was spending the time doing mental gymnastics and Jean-Paul/Mike suddenly looked nervous. Might as well wrap this up. I realized I had another stop to make today.

"Well, when I hear back about the menu adjustments, I will let you know. You might want to stop by the police and see if you can get your side in before they have to drag you," I offered.

"Wait … you're still going to hire me?" he replied with a shocked look.

"Of course … good caterers are hard to find." I mean really … who gives up a good caterer?

We finished up and I noticed he left The Resort. I guess he wasn't in the mood to talk to Jess anymore, which meant I could chorale her.

~~~

I walked back into Jess's office as she was finishing up on the phone. She was making notes about something and nodding a lot. She hung up and put a finger up while she made more notes. I knew better than to interrupt her train of thought so I waited.

"What's up? I would have thought you were tired of this place by now?"

"Actually, I need help only you can give me."

"Do tell."

"I need to talk to whoever was on the front desk the morning of the wedding? Do you know who it was?"

"Yeah, I mean, I'll confirm first. But why the morning?"

"I just have to confirm a few things. I don't quite have it nailed down where the players were." Under other circumstances, I might have gotten another lecture on not getting involved, but I noticed the cover up was heavy this morning, which meant she wasn't sleeping. So being a suspect really was bothering her no matter her protestations.

We walked out to the lobby and luckily it wasn't busy. When we got there, Jess walked over to the check-in desk and talked to a shorter middle-aged man in a navy suit. His name tag said "Beau." They both walked over to where I was waiting off to the side.

"Maddy, this is Beau, he was on duty the morning of the Barton-

Franklin wedding. He is one of our longest employees, and an excellent ambassador for the Lake Wilson Resort and Spa," Jess introduced us. She laid it on a little thick, but I think she wanted to reassure him that he wasn't in trouble or at least wasn't going to get in trouble for talking to me.

"It's nice to meet you, Beau."

"It is a pleasure to meet you, Ms. Carson. The wedding was beautiful, you both did a lovely job." So, he knew who I was.

"I know this might seem somewhat odd, Beau, but I had a few questions about the morning of the wedding. Before everyone left for the ceremony," I said.

"It was pretty quiet since we didn't have many check-outs that morning. I'm not sure how much I can help," he replied.

"I just have a few questions." Beau nodded. "Were there any members of the wedding party down in the lobby before they left for the church?" I asked.

He obviously was thinking it over and didn't knee jerk answer. That made me feel somewhat better. At least I knew he was giving the question some thought.

"Yes, there were a few. The bride came down pretty early and stopped in the gift shop. But she went right back into the elevator when she was done in there. The groom and one of the groomsmen came down and went for a run and returned about an hour later. Mrs. Barton came down looking for Tylenol. I directed her to the gift shop. I don't believe I saw when she left or where she went. One of the groomsmen came down and was looking for a place to smoke. I informed him there was a smoking patio reserved for guests out back. Then a Mr. Bergstrom came in wanting to know where the wedding party was. I explained we didn't give out guest information but called up to the suite for him. He was looking for one of the bridesmaids. A few minutes later, she came down, or I'm assuming it was her, and they went outside for a little while. When she came back, alone, she went straight to the elevator. But that is all I can recall off hand," he replied. That was far more detail then I was hoping to get.

"That is a fairly detailed recall, Beau," I said. "How do you remember all of that?" I was truly impressed.

"Well, we don't have a dedicated concierge so I try to take note of these things, particularly for guests who are here for one of the events. I have always believed in providing the best service possible here at The Resort." He nodded at Jess.

"Thank you for all your help, Beau, you can go back to work now. Sorry to have kept you." I thanked him. He nodded again and walked back to the desk as Jess and I headed back to her office. When we got there, she closed the door.

"Did that help?" she asked.

"Yeah, it did. But where do you find employees with that kind of recall?" I was still amazed he could remember that.

"Beau is a throwback. I keep trying to get him made concierge but the owners aren't sure they want to create the position. We have a couple of employees like that. I really think it would help if guests had someone like him helping them with plans, reservations, things like that," she replied.

"Well, push harder."

I gave her a hug and made my way out. It was a beautiful day and I still had daylight to burn. I wondered how Roger was doing.

Chapter Fourteen

As I sat in my car at The Resort, I started to wonder how what I had learned fit and how it led to Rodney dying. How does Rodney fit in with real estate development and property transactions? And who would want to run Roger down?

I didn't want to get anyone fired over asking about Roger's status, but that didn't mean I couldn't call as a concerned citizen and see if he was okay. Maybe they could at least tell me if he was alive. I went ahead and dialed the number to the hospital and figured I had nothing to lose.

"Lake Wilson Medical Center," a very cheery voice answered. "This is Melinda, how may I direct your call?"

"Hi Melinda, my name is Maddy Carson. I was there this morning when Roger Atkins was picked up by the ambulance. I just wanted to be transferred to his room to see how he is doing."

"Oh, hi, Ms. Carson. It's Melinda Becker, I was in school with MJ. Mr. Atkins isn't out of surgery yet. I'm not sure what floor he will be put on."

"Oh, Melinda, I didn't recognize your voice. Well, I hope Roger gets out of surgery soon and is fine. I will call back later and check on him. How's your family doing?" It couldn't hurt to be nice. If I was remembering correctly, Melinda was a pleasant enough girl and had never done anything to warrant me being rude.

"They are fine, Ms. Carson. Thank you for asking. How's MJ? I think

I heard he was in Europe somewhere."

"He is. He's working on his Master's in England. He's enjoying himself. I'll let him know you asked. How are you liking working at the hospital?"

"I like it well enough. I'm going to TCCC. I haven't quite figured out what I want to do yet. But I'm sure I'll figure it out soon enough." Melinda sounded remarkably grounded and practical for someone so young. I might have to remember her next time MJ came home. Not that I would ever play matchmaker. Okay, who was I kidding? I would in a second.

"Well, thank you for your help, Melinda. I'll just try back later."

"Bye, Ms. Carson."

Well, that wasn't as productive as I hoped, but it did tell me that whatever happened this morning was more serious then I first guessed. At least serious enough to warrant surgery. Maybe they were just setting his leg? I hoped it was something that straight forward. And something that didn't interfere with his ability to remember, because like it or not, he and I were going to have to have another talk.

Just because Roger wasn't holding court over the bank didn't mean that it was closed. I mean, who better than your co-workers to know what you are working on? So I headed toward the Lake Wilson Savings and Loan, affectionately called "the Bank" in our town, as we didn't have many. As I was pulling into the parking lot, Lucy Barton was pulling out. I waved to be friendly but either she didn't see me or didn't care because she pulled out without waving back.

When I walked in, I realized all of the tellers were crying. I guess Roger was more popular with his staff than he was with those he considered beneath him. See, I'm quick like that and I don't think I had ever seen a bank teller anywhere crying in a bank. Unless it was being robbed, of course. And I had never actually seen that since I've never been in a bank robbery before. But that is beside the point. I walked over to one of the tellers I knew and waited for her to compose herself.

"What's wrong, Susan?" I asked while handing her a Kleenex. I never knew why the bank had Kleenex at the teller stands … mystery solved.

"It's just horrible, Ms. Carson, Roger was hit by a car this morning. We couldn't figure out why he was late and then the police came in and told us. It's horrible," she explained. She was on the verge of another crying fit and no one seemed to have the first idea of what to do. I pulled Susan over to one of the customer service chairs and got her situated with more Kleenex.

"Oh, I'm so sorry, that is horrible," I tried to console her. "I'm sure he'll be fine." How I knew that I had no clue but isn't that what you say in these situations? There was no need to make myself the center of attention by disclosing I had seen the whole thing.

"I'm sure he will … it's all just such a shock," and she wailed again.

"Let me go get you a cup of tea or some water. I'm sure that will help," I offered. I turned and noticed Roger's office door was open. I was sure he had a Keurig or some water in there. He had customers in all the time, so it just made sense. And that is what I told myself as I walked in and closed the door most of the way. I made my way over to his desk and was surprised to see how neat and orderly it was. I don't know what I was expecting but it wasn't this much organization. And not quite this much business if truth be told.

There were land transfer deeds and mortgage paperwork on his desk. Not surprisingly, it was mostly related to land up by Lake Wilson. I guess that made sense, after the bank did lots of buying and selling and transferring after all. You can't make millions on development deals if you don't own all the land. So everyone was selling their land to the developers who were building luxury homes and then doing all the work to find homeowners. There were also deposit slips for clients. I probably shouldn't be privy to them but they were mostly for companies and trusts, not individuals.

What did strike me was Roger's name on some of the transfer paperwork. I guess he really was getting a chance to play with the big boys. Hmmm … I thought it was all talk. Whatever he was part of, it was a lot of land being passed around, he was right in the middle of it. If Rodney was blackmailing people, he really did have a wealth of knowledge at his disposal. And if Roger was this involved it made you wonder if his getting run over was connected to Rodney's death.

"Well, I wasn't expecting to find you here," came a voice from the door. A voice I knew and had known since high school. Nick Carletti had caught me red handed. But red handed doing what? Being nosy? Welcome to Lake Wilson.

"I was getting Susan some water," I explained. Luckily, there was bottled water in a cute little triangle formation. Unluckily, it was on the credenza by the door, not on the desk.

"Well, that was nice of you but were you taking the scenic route?" he asked snarkily. Yeah, I had that one coming.

"I was just shocked to hear about Roger and was trying to figure out why someone might do that," I offered. That wasn't going to help me but at least I was being honest. Brownie points for that, right?

"Well, that's my job. You can help by staying out of my way," he added as he motioned me out of the office. I took a last look around as I grabbed a bottle of water and caught a picture of Roger and Rodney together at some kind of picnic. It was taken years ago, probably during college. They looked happy and carefree.

We had made it back to Susan and I handed her the water and patted her shoulder.

"Can I get you anything else?"

"No, Ms. Carson. Thank you so much. I'm sorry. Did you need something? I'm sure you didn't come in to comfort me." Nick stood looking at me and seemed very interested in my answer.

"Well, yes, actually. I was hoping to get a chance to talk to Roger about something. But obviously he isn't around. Is the assistant manager in?" I hoped I sounded like I had actual bank business to discuss.

"Steven Treeves? Yes, he is in his office. The one with the closed door. Between us, I'm not sure he knows what to do with Mr. Atkins not here to tell him."

I looked at Nick, hoping that maybe, just maybe, he believed I had actual bank business today. And in some ways, I did. It just wasn't my bank business. I got up, made sure Susan was okay, and walked toward Steven Treeves closed door. Nick stayed with Susan but he did watch me walk away. I knocked on the door and he invited me in.

"Mr. Treeves, I just wondered if you had a moment?"

"I'm sorry. Yes, of course I do for a loyal customer. How can I help you, Ms. Carson." I looked through my internal rolodex and tried to figure out what I knew about Steven Treeves. He was a few years ahead of Megan in high school. He had always been best described as average. Average height, average weight, average personality. He was the top of the bell curve. Not that there was anything wrong with that. Someone has to be there, actually almost half the population was there. For all I knew, others would consider me average. But Steven Treeves just struck me as the poster child for, well, average.

"I just had a few questions, Mr. Treeves, about some new investment opportunities Roger had mentioned to me the other night." No need to tell him that he hadn't actually mentioned me taking part in those investments.

"Please, call me Steven," he replied. "What investments were those? We don't offer many new options. I mean, there's the same programs we offered when you opened your accounts, Ms. Carson. Did he happen to mention what the investments were or what they involved?" he asked.

"I think he mentioned something about the Lake Wilson developments. I'm not sure specifically what they were concerning."

"Ahhh. Well, that explains it. Those investments aren't being handled through the bank. The board does not wish to get involved with that kind of speculation. I mean, we are assisting with the closings when a member sells property but that is as far as it goes. Do you have any property up at the lake you are planning on unloading?"

"No, my family never extended out to the lake. We were always in the town." Just then, there was a knock at the door and Nick peeked in. He looked at both of us and then came in.

"I'm sorry, I hope I'm not interrupting anything." Oh, I just bet he was. He wasn't sorry at all.

"No, I was just finished."

"Well, if you remember anything else about those investments, Ms. Carson, please, let me know. I'll be happy to help you if I can," he offered.

"Investments?" Nick asked. Although, could you really ask a question with one word?

"Yes, Ms. Carson was interested in potential investment opportunities we offer. But unfortunately we don't offer any related to the Lake Wilson Development. At least not at this time," he explained.

"Land speculation, Maddy? You didn't strike me as the type." Nick was smirking at me. He was, I swear he was. Why couldn't I have been involved in land speculation? I could speculate with the best of them. Okay, maybe I didn't want to point that out aloud.

"I'll need to speak to you, Mr. Treeves. But first, I'll just walk Ms. Carson to her car."

"That's okay, Detective, I can manage without assistance." I really didn't need to talk to him right now. I had too many questions I knew he wouldn't answer.

"Think nothing of it, Ms. Carson." Great, now I would look rude if I refused. Nick put his hand on my back and ushered me out the door and toward my car. I was hoping he would just let me get in and leave without comment, but I had never been that lucky.

"Maddy, I thought we talked about this. I thought I made it clear you weren't to get involved with this investigation." He sounded frustrated with me. And I could kind of, sort of, see his point. Almost. But his best friend wasn't on the short list for suspects.

"I'm not sure what you are talking about?"

"You, in Roger Atkin's office. And talking to wedding guests and the caterer?"

"We never discussed my not asking questions about Roger's accident. Heck, I haven't seen you since he was hit. And I'm allowed to ask about feedback from people who have attended an event I worked." That sounded weak even to me.

"You are doing more than that and you know it. You have to stay out of it."

"I would if you would assure me you were not looking at Jess anymore. Can you do that?" I probably could step back if he would just reassure me that Jess was no longer a suspect.

"I am not discussing an ongoing investigation with you. You are a member of the public and nothing more." His voice was starting to raise and I realized I may have pushed too far.

"Well then, since I'm just a member of the public, I guess I'll have to go see how Roger is doing and ask him how he could have possibly found a phone in Rod's apartment that wasn't there hours before. Or what Rod was going to do with land development information? Or what any of the people who were supposed to be getting ready for the wedding but were traipsing around all over the ground floor might have seen that morning?" Now my voice was raising. This was quickly going to hit argument level and I hate having arguments. He suddenly looked at me with a mild level of shock.

"Where did you get all of that from?" he asked.

"People talk to me. I'm generally considered a pleasant person. Don't they talk to you? I mean, since you're Mr. Charming Personality and all." I couldn't help the jab. I was annoyed.

"Well, stop asking. You could seriously jeopardize my case. I don't want to have to arrest you. Why don't you just tell me what it is you have running around in your head." I guess this was his version of a peace offering.

"Okay, fine. We'll try it your way. What does a wannabe monk who gives half his paycheck to animal shelters do with land development information? I mean, he doesn't have the capital to buy land and he doesn't have the connections to set up a deal. And how is it that Sarah, Roger, and Jean-Paul all had the chance to kill Rodney before the wedding, but you haven't cleared Jess? I mean, we have to know that someone else was the mastermind behind the college scam, and he knew both Sarah and Roger then. Does Jean-Paul still have mob connections and maybe he's doing something with the development transactions? After all, aren't mobsters always involved in construction and such? And who ran Roger over? Because there is no way that was a coincidence. Has anyone asked Sarah and Jean-Paul where they were? Because Jess was at work already. That alone should clear her of any involvement." I think that was pretty much it. Maybe it was overkill, but he asked.

"Wow. That's a lot. Do you have that much running around in your head all day? Or was that accumulated?"

"I have more, but it's not related to the murder. My head is like an internet browser. I always have a ton of tabs open. That's just one of them. Stop avoiding the topic. Is Jess cleared?"

"As much as I would love to get you focused on one of your other 'tabs,' I don't discuss on going investigations with members of the public." He really was one of the most frustrating people ever. On the one hand, I found it commendable he wouldn't compromise his policy just to get me off his back. On the other hand, why couldn't he just put my mind at ease? Was it that big a deal?

"Then don't ask me to stop being a concerned friend who is doing her due diligence on quality control for recent projects I've worked on. An event coordinator's job is never done." With that, I got in my car and left Nick Carletti standing in the parking lot.

Chapter Fifteen

The next day, I was sitting at my desk trying to distract myself when I realized I wasn't going to be able to get anything done until I got to talk to Roger Atkins. I caved and called the hospital. When I asked for his room this time they connected me to the nurse's station where they informed me he was sleeping and he had requested not to be disturbed. Well, at least I knew he was out of surgery. But before I went to visit him, I had one stop to make.

I pulled up in front of A Cut Above thirty minutes later and hoped I could catch Gwen between clients. I walked in and saw her finishing up on a sleek bob. She looked at me and motioned me over.

"What's up? Did I forget about an event or something?" she asked.

"Nope, I just needed to talk to you when you've got a moment," I replied.

"In that case, just take a seat in my office. I'll be there in a minute."

I moved back to Gwen's office, which was just as comfy and homey as the rest of the shop. It was decorated in soft grays and family photos. Gwen and her husband Darren had been married forever and had five kids. Looking at the photos it was clear they were a tight knit family.

"So, what's up, girl?" Gwen asked as she walked in and sat in her desk chair.

"I hope I'm not interrupting anything. Are you sure you have time?" I really didn't want to take her away from customers.

"We're good. I had a cancellation and I don't have another appointment for an hour. So, what's up?"

"I know we talked about it, but I wanted to ask you about the morning of the wedding. I just need to figure some things out." I explained.

"Sure, but I'm not sure how much help I'll be. I was up to my elbows in hairspray and up-dos."

"I just need to see what you may remember. Specifically, did Sarah or Lucy leave the suite at any time?" I didn't want her memory to be influenced by what Beau had told me so I figured I wouldn't mention what I had been told.

"Well, that's easy enough. Sarah was MIA for a while because she was holding everyone up. She had insisted on some chignon that belonged in the 50s but then we couldn't find her. When she finally came back, she was flushed and out of breath. I know Neal Bergstrom was blowing up her phone and finally called the suite. Lucy was fit to be tied that he was being such a nuisance. But she was another one who we had to wait on. She had complained about a headache and went in search of Tylenol. You would think, when everyone is getting ready for a wedding of all things, people wouldn't disappear. What the hell is wrong with people?"

"Wait, how long was Lucy out of the suite?" I asked.

"At least a half an hour. She left while I was working on the maid of honor and didn't come back until I was done with her and we were waiting for her. Stacy was fit to be tied. After all the fuss her mom made for this big show she couldn't be found."

"That's crazy. Did she say what she was doing?"

"She just said something about double checking on things. But at that point, we were running late and so I was hustling. Because you know damn well that she would have given me crap for running late and not have taken any responsibility for it." She wasn't wrong about that.

"Okay, thanks."

"So, what's going on? Why all the questions?" Gwen knew Jess and I and we had all been friendly for years.

"Well, the cops put Jess on the short list and while she's handling it well, but I know it's bothering her. And honestly, someone killing Rod just offends me. I mean, he was a good guy. He was making a new life and had a future planned. He was helping and not bothering people. I know it's not what the cops believe, but what they are looking at doesn't fit. I just feel like they aren't looking where they should."

"You're not going to do the locker room thing again, are you?" she asked.

"Why does everyone bring that up? You get stuck in one locker and it follows you forever," I said defensively.

"You have to admit, it was funny," she laughed. I was so glad my high school humiliation could still make people laugh thirty years later. And then, I started laughing, too.

"All right, I'll get out of your hair," I said while standing up and heading out.

"Hair pun ... you're cute."

I was heading out to my car when Nick pulled up next to me. I leaned against my car as he got out and walked over. He was dressed in what I was beginning to think of as his "detective uniform," a boring suit and tie.

"Good morning, Detective Carletti," I greeted. *And there goes the eyebrow.*

"Morning, Maddy. I think it can just be Nick, don't you? I mean, we're friends."

"Are we?" I asked.

"Yes, Maddy, we are. It's just right now I have a job to do and you don't like it very much. But I'm not the enemy."

"What I don't like is my best friend worried she could be arrested for something she clearly would never do." I don't know why it was so important for me to convince him that she was innocent. For him to believe me about her.

"If it's any consolation she's pretty low on the list, but that's as much as I'm telling you, Maddy. Seriously. You need to let me do my job."

"Well, that's a tiny bit difficult right now," I said.

"Why?" he asked.

"Because I think I might know who did it. And how. And maybe even why. But I can't prove it. I need somethings verified. I mean, it would be slander, right? If I accused someone and they didn't do it?" I was rambling now. But then again I was nervous.

"Well, I guess it could be, but I'm pretty sure you should tell me and let me handle it."

"Ummm ... I'm pretty sure that might be right, but again, the slander thing. I mean, isn't slander worse when it's to a police officer?" There was no way he was going to leave me out of this. I wasn't leaving it up to him when I had to ask questions. After all, what if he didn't ask the right ones?

"You're not going to let this go, are you?" he asked.

I shook my head. I mean, this way later I could say I hadn't actually said I wouldn't. Plausible deniability was my friend.

"Fine, but you and I are doing this together. You are not going off by yourself. And if I tell you to stay in the car or to leave then you do it. Got it?" I had to admit, Nick in authoritative cop mode was kind of hot.

"Got it." I really was tempted to salute, but I didn't think he would appreciate it at all.

We pulled up to the hospital ten minutes later and Nick walked us to the information desk and asked for Roger's room number. I'm not sure they would have let me in without his badge. I guess having a police escort was helpful. We stopped right outside Roger's door. He was lying in bed in a hospital gown with a bandage on his head. His leg was elevated and wrapped from hip to toe. Ouch. That didn't look comfortable. But he was awake … that was good … I could work with awake. Nick grabbed the door handle and then changed his mind and stopped us.

"Listen, I'm only letting you do this because it seems like you have an idea of what is going on, but you do anything to compromise an arrest and I'm going to have you banned from this hospital," he threatened. He was obviously waiting for me to agree. Of course, I was going to. And he really needed to be more specific. How would I know what would compromise an arrest?

"Okay, fair enough," I agreed. After all, I didn't think we would be here that long. And it wasn't my job to catch a murderer.

"Detective Carletti and Maddy, to what do I owe the honor? I thought I had answered all the officer's questions before, Detective." Roger looked at us skeptically. Nick crossed his arms and leaned against the door and it was obvious he wasn't going to say anything. He wasn't really sure what to say, I guess. This was, after all, my circus.

"I was just wondering, Roger, why you would frame your brother for blackmail and cover up for his killer?" I stated. I guess I wasn't going to do subtle today.

"What the hell are you talking about, Madeline Carson?" He had the good sense to look offended as he sat up straighter. But really, the full name was reserved for my mother and Mrs. Carletti so that just ticked me off.

"I didn't realize it until I saw a picture of you and your brother together. You're not just twins, your identical twins. And that's when I realized that from behind you would be virtually indistinguishable. Especially if you were both wearing tuxedoes. Your brother wasn't the intended victim at the wedding … you were. And when you realized that someone you were blackmailing had killed him, you set it up to make it look like he did the blackmailing. Were you hoping to fool the murderer into believing they were safe or just protect yourself from the cops?" I really was curious as to his motive.

In the minute that followed, it was obvious Roger was debating whether to play innocent or come clean. But when you are in a hospital bed because someone tried to kill you, playing innocent is going to be a hard sell. He took a deep breath, and you could see his shoulders relax. I knew we might get some answers from him now. He laid his head back on the raised bed and blew out the breath he had been holding.

"From the cops. I mean, I figured it was easier to pin it on him then to leave it a loose end. I wasn't really worried about anyone going to the police, but I had no clue what they would find. And if they did catch his killer then it would definitely come out. I didn't feel good about it or anything. But I guess I was used to him protecting me," he said defeatedly.

"You mean because he took the rap for the college scam instead of telling the police of your involvement?" I had already worked that out.

"How did you know that?" He looked shocked. Even Nick looked a little surprised at that one. He had done well with the poker face so far. Or maybe he knew this, and I was stepping on his toes, but I didn't think so. I looked at Nick and shrugged. It made sense when you thought about it. I mean, who else would you take that kind of hit for besides family?

"There was no way he would have come up with that by himself. And they threw the book at him for not naming his partner. There aren't many people you would take a bullet for, but your brother? Yeah, you'll take a bullet for them. What I don't have figured out is how did you know about Sarah and Mike?" I asked. This was the part I had no concrete theories about. I had hunches, but I didn't *know* anything.

"I saw Sarah when I went to visit Rod while he was working in the strip club a few times. She was dancing. She had an amazing body. Still does under those prim and proper dresses. When she came into the bank to open an account, I knew I recognized her, but it took a while to remember where from. Mike I had seen in the visitor's room when I went to visit Rod. They served time at the same prison. When he came here as Jean-Paul or whatever the hell he was calling himself, I didn't think anything of it. Then he got jobs working for the developers and I couldn't believe my luck. It was like a sign or something," he offered as some kind of lame defense.

"So, you got the information on what land and when it would be bought and how high the developers were willing to go," I summarized.

"Yup, it all worked so perfectly. I knew I could maximize how much I made and keep them coming back for more because I had connections. It was all so simple, and I made a killing on the land," he finished.

"But you don't own land," Nick added. "How were you going to make anything?" he asked.

"That's where Lucy Barton comes in," I stated.

"Lucy Barton?" Nick looked genuinely confused now.

"Yes, Lucy. I noticed that Roger had deeds from L.O. Ltd. and Founding Fathers Trust on his desk moving land around and selling it. I have to imagine she had her family's land and sold it to L.O. Ltd. to get her husband's name off it. Then when Roger realized what she was doing, he threatened to tell her husband unless he cut her in. Now that Stacy was married and on her way, Lucy wanted out of her marriage and made plans to live a bigger life then she was allowed before," I filled in the holes.

"But how does L.O. Ltd. and Founding Fathers give you all that?" Nick demanded.

"Lucy Barton wasn't always Lucy Barton. Her maiden name is Lucy Oxmoor … L.O. And I figure the Founding Fathers jab was Roger's way of putting her in her place. She's always throwing it around that her family has been here since the dawn of time. Or at least the dawn of Lake Wilson. When L.O. Ltd. transferred half its land to Founding Fathers, he got what he wanted and took a dig at Lucy." I looked at Roger as if to ask for confirmation.

"Yeah, that's pretty much how it was. She always looked down at those of us who hadn't been here for a hundred years. It was getting old. I noticed she sold land to her LLC from her joint account for $1 and figured she was up to something. She kept the LLC account at our bank. It wasn't hard to look up the land transfer. It's all public record. I didn't know about the maiden name thing, but had seen her open an individual account and start depositing money in it after land sales. Then I noticed L.O. Ltd. was listed on some of that land that was in Sarah's information. Didn't take a rocket scientist to put it together. With the information I had, Lucy made a killing. I just wanted my share," he reasoned.

"Yeah, but none of it was really your share, Roger, and she was upset, wasn't she?" I explained. "She couldn't have the whole thing come out. If her husband found out then her plans for divorce would get much more complicated," I continued, looking at Nick.

"And Rodney wanted me to put a stop to the whole plan. We argued that morning in the ballroom. He wanted me to confess and return the money and land. He wanted to tell Sarah and Jean-Paul the truth. He actually thought I should go to the police. He was always so idealistic. I told him we would discuss it after the wedding. I figured I might be able to talk him out of it," Roger explained.

"So, how does that get us to Rod's murder?" Nick wanted it all now.

"Roger wasn't there for that. We need to get to Lucy's. I would bet she emptied her accounts and is planning on leaving soon. You should call for a look out or whatever it is," I said, waving at him. "But I'll bet she's at her house and we can catch her. She shouldn't be leaving until tomorrow at the earliest."

"How do you figure?" Nick raised that eyebrow again.

"Stacy comes home tomorrow. She'll want to say goodbye. It would be rude to not welcome her back," I answered like it was the most obvious thing in the world.

Chapter Sixteen

Lucy lived about twenty minutes from the hospital in a newer McMansion development. The kind where everyone has crown molding and granite countertops but less than a half-acre per lot. I figured Nick would have a few questions on the way, but it threw me for a loop when he brought up the blackmail instead of the murder.

"So, how did you know Rodney wasn't the one blackmailing everyone?" Nick pressed. He was remarkably calm for someone on their way to confront a murderer. That is probably what made him the cop and me the event coordinator. I wonder if his texting in the elevator was to make sure Lucy didn't leave town?

"From what everyone said he wasn't the brains behind the whole college scam. It seemed that this whole blackmailing scheme required at least that much brain power. I mean, using Sarah and Mike/Jean-Paul was pretty smart as far as getting inside information. Rod didn't have that kind of deviousness in him. I mean, he spent his free time volunteering at animal shelters, not studying real estate listing. It just didn't fit. Even his parole officer thought he was going straight, and he's jaded," I explained. I didn't want to mention that there was nothing in his apartment indicating he was a criminal mastermind or real estate genius. "Besides, Rod didn't own a cell phone. It's disruptive of a peaceful life."

"And Roger handing in the phone gave it away," he assumed. We were interrupted by Nick's phone ringing. He instructed the officers to pull up a few houses down and not do anything until he got there.

"That was stupid. I mean, if you believed Rod could blackmail people then I guess lying about owning a cell phone wouldn't be hard, but why lie about it? If Roger hadn't turned the phone in, I'm not sure anyone would have known about the blackmail. Sarah and Mike weren't going to say a word. I think he was more worried about Lucy and figured it would keep her off his back," I speculated. It struck me as sloppy. But then again, I had never blackmailed anyone, so maybe Roger was always worried someone would find out. I would have been.

As we pulled into Lucy's development, Nick finally got to the bigger question.

"But how does that get you to Lucy committing murder?" he asked.

"She was desperate, and desperate people will do anything to get out of their dilemma, real or imagined. She had been looking forward to starting over and moving on from her marriage so that anything that got in her way was just an obstacle that needed to be removed. She had been planning on starting her life over, or at least recreating herself, for months. And then Roger Atkins of all people got in her way. No, she wasn't going to take that," I wrapped up as we pulled into her driveway enough to block her exit. As we walked to the door and rang the bell, I suddenly realized I had no idea how this would play out.

Lucy opened it after Nick rang the doorbell a second time. I don't know what I was expecting but a cheerful Lucy wasn't it. She looked mildly annoyed as if we had interrupted her but quickly put on a smiling hostess face. I don't know where Reginald was, but I figured he was at work as it was a weekday. If I was right, there were probably half-packed suitcases lying open on her bed.

"Detective Carletti, Maddy, what are you two doing here?" Lucy asked. I have to admit she didn't strike me as someone who had tried to run over Roger and killed Rodney. It wasn't until now that I noticed the change in appearance that Gwen had mentioned. Her hair was cut in a more updated style and her wardrobe had a major overhaul. She looked ten years younger than I was used to seeing.

"I just have a couple of follow up questions if you don't mind, Mrs. Barton," Nick answered as he walked in the door without an invite. Lucy, ever gracious, led us toward the formal living room. She motioned for us to sit on the couch while she took a seat in one of the upholstered chairs sitting across from us. I noticed she didn't offer coffee so she might be cracking after all. At the very least, she didn't want us staying too long.

"Of course, but I'm not sure why Maddy is here." She looked at me rather pointedly. What was it that had people dismissing me so rudely? I mean, I know I wasn't a police officer, but really. Manners people.

"Well, Maddy has an interesting theory and I just thought it would be easier to explore if we all put our heads together," he replied. Great, he was leaving this to me again.

"Oh really?" She turned her attention to me. Again, a handbook in this situation would be really helpful. But I figured direct had worked with Roger so I might as well try it again.

"I just had a question, Lucy. Did you have Sarah's bracelet on you when you killed Rodney or did you come back and drop it later?" I asked. This was one of the small items that had been bugging me.

"Whatever are you talking about?" Lucy laughed. I think she would have clutched her pearls if she had been wearing them. The laugh didn't quite make it to her eyes though and that's when I realized I knew exactly what had happened.

"Well, let me see if I can lay it all out and you can let me know where I'm wrong? You and the wedding party were getting ready in the bridal suite. For some reason you decided to go down to the lobby. Maybe you were looking for aspirin or just needed a break, I'm not sure why, but it doesn't matter now. You went down to the lobby. You noticed Roger walking into the ballroom. After talking to the desk clerk and going to the gift shop, you decided to confront Roger. I'm not sure when you entered the ballroom but all you saw was Roger, or who you thought was Roger, from the back and he was walking back toward the closet. You were so angry about him taking half of the proceeds of the secret land sale that you just wanted to make him pay. You picked up the cherub because it was right there and hit him over the head. When he fell, you realized it was Rodney, the wrong brother, and panicked. You took one of the tablecloths to wipe off your prints and wrapped up the cherub and dropped it in the dumpster out the back door. It was probably propped open for deliveries. On the way out you saw staff, so you pretended to be there checking on the place settings and decorations. You then went back to the suite and got ready and waited for someone to find the body," I explained.

"I needed an aspirin," Lucy added after a minute of silence. "All those dim-witted flighty girls were giving me a headache. Talking about how wonderful marriage is without having a clue. I went to the lobby and saw Roger go to the ballroom. I went to the front desk asking for aspirin but he just pointed me to the gift shop and by then I had worked myself up. Who did Roger think he was? He was nobody and he was taking what was rightfully mine away. How dare he?" She was working herself up again.

"When I walked into the ballroom, I thought it was him heading back to the bathroom area. Turns out Roger had left through the French doors to join the groomsmen for pictures but I didn't know that. I didn't mean to hurt Rodney ... I swear. But his brother was taking my last chance away." She sat down looking broken. I almost felt bad for her.

"But I don't understand. It wasn't just yours ... the land that is. It was in both yours and your husband's names. You hadn't told him about the sale?" I wanted to know what her motivation was. She was so angry even now.

"IT WAS MINE!!! My father had been stupid enough to leave it to both of us in his will, but it was mine and I wasn't giving it up to anyone," she raged, standing up. I leaned back and Nick got up and walked over to her. He placed a hand on her shoulder and tried to push her back into her seat.

"Easy, Mrs. Barton, just sit down and explain it to us." His demeanor became calm and reassuring. This had to be something they taught you in the police academy.

"The land was from MY family. He had no legacy here. His family only moved here in the 1950s. You understand, Maddy, he wasn't invested in our town. We have a responsibility to set an example for the people in this community. If I had told him, he would have invested it in mutual funds or even pushed us to retire to Florida. Florida of all places, can you believe it? No, I was going to be able to divorce him and take my name back and be a scion. A scion," she finally finished and sat back on the couch.

"And the bracelet?"

"I had found it after Sarah left our house. I meant to return it at the reception but decided I would drop it in the hall. At least point the police in a direction away from me. Besides, let's see the Bergstroms have a wedding when the bride is in shackles." Okay, that was just low.

Nick walked Lucy back toward the front door and let the officers in. Lucy had started to cry and looked broken. I almost felt sorry for her. Except for her being a killer and all. By now, Scott had joined us. He read Lucy her rights and allowed the officers to cuff her and take her out to a squad car.

"Is that all of it?" Nick asked.

"Yes, that's it." I responded.

"Good," he said.

I got up and we walked out to his car. We didn't say anything as he drove me back to mine. I promised to come in the next day and give a statement. He was going to be busy for the rest of the day taking statements and figuring out the details but that was all police business.

Chapter Seventeen

I had sworn that I would never step into this place again after I divorced Mitch, but here I was. I didn't tell Nick, but there was something bothering me about the land scheme. Nothing that would impact his arrest or the murder case. But things didn't quite add up the way they should. And really, I was secretly hoping I was wrong.

"Mr. Brodsky will see you now, Ms. Carson," the receptionist said. I wasn't sure if she knew who I was, but the fact that I could see Mitch without an appointment had probably made her just a little curious.

"Thank you."

I walked into Mitch's office and noticed it had been redecorated. I know it had been a while since I had been here, but it was clear it had Heather's stamp all over it. There was no way the Mitch I knew would have picked Louis XIV chairs. If he even knew who Louis XIV was. History never was his strong suit.

"Maddy, what can I do for you? Is there something wrong?" Mitch knew if it had been about the kids, I would have called immediately so I can imagine he was just as curious as his receptionist right about now.

"No. Not really. I wanted to let you know that Lucy Barton has been arrested for Rodney Staltz's murder."

"Okay, but why would that concern me? Or at least enough to warrant a visit from you?" Mitch may not have been a history fan, but he wasn't stupid.

He knew I wouldn't stop by for idle chit chat.

"Well, it's not directly related. But Roger Atkins will also be facing charges." There it was. I saw the slight twitch. Most people wouldn't have seen it but most people hadn't known Mitch for almost thirty years.

"Again, not sure how that relates to me." He wasn't going to give an inch.

"Really? I would think that your source of inside information on the Lake Wilson development project being charged with a felony would at least be a little interesting to you," I said.

"I don't know what you're talking about." Okay, he was going to hold strong.

"Remember what we used to do with the kid's Christmas lists? What your one rule was for the holidays? We weren't allowed to write it down. At least not spell it out. Code was fine, but no lists with their names at the top. I thought it was smart at the time. I mean, we were partners in crime and who wants to get caught with the plan laid out in black and white? You should have taught Roger the same lesson, Mitch." And that's when he knew. Or at least he knew I knew something. His head dropped for a moment and then he looked back up at me.

"He wrote it down? That moron." That was as much of a confession as I would ever get from him. And if there was anyone else in the room we would never have gotten that.

"He wrote it down. He used a few nicknames, but he also used initials. And notes about what he told M.B. and what M.B. told him to do were all over his desk. Not that you actually broke any laws, but that was hardly on the up and up, was it?" I was shocked when I saw his initials on Roger's desk, but I couldn't think of anyone else it could be. Especially when Mitch had mentioned the development at the wedding.

"But why? I mean, really, Mitch, this is small potatoes for you. A local land project? You don't have any land up there and that deal wouldn't be enough to get you out of bed most days. What the hell were you doing getting involved with a small fish like Roger Atkins?" I really had no clue what he was doing.

"It was Heather. She wanted her own career. She wanted to make a go of the design business. She would never make it in the city or up against professionals. But if I could get her in a few of the new homes, or even working on the models, I figured that would be enough to make her happy.

When Roger came to me with his sales pitch, I figured I could get her in that way. I didn't want to do any favors for the developers. They were small time, and I wasn't giving them an in to the big leagues on my tailcoats. But I knew if Roger got what he wanted out of this he would owe me. I just advised him. I provided guidance to someone just starting out. That was all."

"Did you know about the blackmail?" I needed to know. For some reason it mattered. I had always hated the business Mitch was in, but he had always been above board. That much I knew.

"What? No. Of course not. Give me some credit, Mads." He only used that name when he was emotional. I had actually insulted him. "I knew it was odd he had the information, but I honestly thought he was sleeping with someone. Not that he would blackmail anyone. I know you say I can be ruthless, but I am not a criminal."

He was right. I did think he was ruthless. But he was scared enough of prison that he wouldn't have broken the law. And Lucy and Roger had been arrested. There was no real benefit to telling anyone about what role Mitch may, or may not, have played in the whole fiasco.

"Fine. I won't tell anyone. You're just lucky Jess didn't get in any trouble over this."

"I know. I would lose out to Jess any day of the week." He managed to say it without rolling his eyes, which was new.

"But that doesn't mean you are getting off Scot-free." I had, after all, been married to the man.

"What?"

"Stop pushing me on Aggie's house. It's mine. I'm keeping it. Figure out something else to do for Heather's business. Tell her it's rat infested for all I care. But you are not getting my house and I don't want to hear another word about it."

"Fine, I'll figure something else out. Don't be surprised if I paint you as the bitch though." He really was a charmer.

"I expect nothing less." And honestly, I didn't care if Heather thought I was evil. We were never going to be friends anyway.

I got up and started toward the door. I didn't really feel the need to observe social niceties with him.

"The vegetarian chef. Think Megan is serious about him?" I wasn't surprised Meg had told Mitch, but I was surprised he asked me. Maybe this was his idea of an olive branch.

"If he makes it through four dates then I think we may have to learn his name. But let's wait and see if she tells MJ. Then we'll know he's a keeper." Mitch nodded in agreement and got back to work. He had dismissed me. I walked out and promised myself I would never come back here, at least not if I could help it.

Chapter Eighteen

That night I met up with Jess, Tommy, and Rob at The Dive. After the day I had, nothing sounded better than drinks and greasy food with my friends. We were at one of the larger tables since the booth was reserved for just the three of us. I was on my second margarita and third potato skin when Nick and Scott walked in. I was sort of surprised to see them there as it wasn't their normal hang out.

"I invited them," Jess supplied as though she read my mind. I looked at her and raised my eyebrow. Ha ... my turn. "I thought it would be good for you to get it all out so you can move on," she explained. "Besides, I wasn't exactly nice to Nick this week so I figured it couldn't hurt since he will be Scott's partner from now on." I leaned my head on her shoulder briefly. I really didn't know what I would do without her.

Scott and Nick ordered and caught up with Tommy and Rob. Mateo joined at some point and sat next to Tommy. Nick looked between the two of them as they kissed hello. I guess he wasn't totally caught up.

"So, someone needs to explain to me why the hell Lucy Barton would have offed Rodney. I'm lost," Mateo asked the table. He was good at addressing the elephant in the room without stepping on toes. And someone needed to start the conversation we all wanted to have.

"Greed and mistaken identity," Nick answered directly. "But I have to admit we were probably focusing on the blackmail to get us to the murderer and not vice versa. Maddy should probably explain how she got there before we did," Nick diverted the explanation to me.

I took a deep breath. I knew how it worked in my head, but would it sound crazy to them?

"It just didn't make sense. None of it made sense. I mean, who would kill Rod and why at a wedding? And him being a blackmailer, that made even less sense," I started. "Nothing anyone said about him got us to that point. Everyone, even his parole officer, believed he was going straight. And he was caring about animals and moving to Tibet. This isn't someone with material goals. I mean, the money could have gotten him there, but it would seem to defeat the whole good karma point thing."

"But why murder someone at your daughter's wedding?" Tommy asked. He had been quiet most of the night. Of everyone at the table, he's the only one who had really known Rodney and it occurred to me that he might have been more upset than I first thought by the whole ordeal. I looked at him with new sympathy. He nodded for me to continue.

"Honestly, I think it was the circumstances. This should have been one of the biggest days of her life. Mother of the bride at the biggest social event of the year in her domain. From what we know now, this was her day to shine as much as Stacy's ... maybe even more so. And she had to listen to a bunch of young girls talking about how wonderful marriage was while she was miserable in hers. And when she escaped, even for a moment, she was faced with the one person who had ruined her plans. I imagine it was all too much," I concluded.

"But how do you confuse Roger and Rodney?" Jess asked.

"I can answer that one," Nick volunteered. Oh, this should be good. I took another sip of my drink and sat back.

"Lucy said she clearly saw Roger enter the ballroom but went to get something from the front desk for her headache. She had worked herself up and decided to confront him before going back to the suite. By the time she went into the ballroom she only saw what it turns out was Rodney, from behind, and followed him not realizing her error. Roger said Rodney was already in the ballroom and caught him and confronted him. They agreed to discuss it after the wedding and went their separate ways, but he knew Rodney wasn't going to stand for it. Roger went out one of the patio doors and Rodney headed back toward the bathrooms and closet," Nick explained.

"When Lucy walked in she followed Rodney back and hit him in a moment of blind rage. When she realized what she had done, and to who, she tried covering it up. When the staff saw her she pretended to be check the table settings and being her usual picky self," Scott picked up. "We knew from the coroner that the killer was shorter than the victim, but that applied to every suspect we had so that wasn't any help."

"When she came in later as part of the reception she stopped and dropped Sarah's bracelet when she went to the ladies' room. Turns out she isn't a big fan of the Bergstroms and was hoping it would ruin Neal and Sarah's wedding planning," Nick explained.

"But what was the end goal? I mean, I thought she and Reginald were a golden couple?" Rob quizzed. He had been quiet the whole night, but that wasn't anything new for him. He always tended to let Jess, Tommy, and I dominate the conversation.

"Turns out she's been miserable for years. According to her, old Reg is cheap and boring. Her words, not mine," Scott answered. "She thought she should have been allowed to live bigger and better than he was comfortable with. She wanted to be the queen bee and he wanted to save for retirement. I guess he started to mention retiring early and moving and she realized she needed out before he ruined her whole life."

"It was just a coincidence Rodney and Roger were in the ballroom at the same time?" I finally asked. It occurred to me I had been out with the groomsman and the photographer when this was all happening. So close and yet clueless.

"Yes, Rod was getting ready to set up and Roger just happened to come in. Rodney stopped him because Mike/Jean-Paul had just confronted him, and Rod knew it had to be Roger's doing. I guess Rod was going to come to us, but Roger convinced him they should talk after the wedding. Rod told Roger he was going to find a quiet place to meditate for a few minutes to get his chi straight or something. I guess that is why he was heading to the closet, no one would interrupt him there."

"Then after Rodney was discovered it was a matter of Roger setting up Rod so he would be in the clear. Roger thought he would be okay but then Lucy ran him down in the street and he realized he was in danger. I think he was getting nervous because Lucy didn't tell anyone she was leaving so he thought she might come after him again. Not sure what he would have done if Maddy hadn't confronted him," Nick finished.

With that, all eyes turned to me. Not sure why … not like there was much more to say. And of course, I had just bitten into a potato skin. I shrugged.

"It was the picture in the office. When I saw the brothers together I realized how much they really looked alike and it all clicked. What if Rodney wasn't the intended victim? What if Roger was, and then it all started to make sense. Whereas Rod didn't fit as a blackmailer, Roger did. He has always been self-centered and money hungry. And whereas I couldn't see how Rod would care about land development, I knew Roger was obsessed with it. It all worked from there," I finished.

Everyone kind of nodded and took a minute. Finally, Tommy asked if we needed another round, which we all agreed we did and topics other than murder and blackmail started to dominate the conversation. It struck me the town as a whole would know all the details soon enough. We were all going to be shook for a while that one of our own had done it but eventually life would go back to normal.

~~~

Everyone had finished their drinks and we were making our way out after saying goodnight to Tommy and Mateo. I gave Jess and Rob hugs and told Jess I would text her tomorrow. I'm pretty sure I would be working all day from home catching up on things. Scott waved off as he headed to his car parked down the street. It left Nick and me.

"Where are you parked?" he asked.

"I'm not. I walked. It's a nice night and it seems like a waste to drive a few blocks," I answered.

"I'll walk you home then. You can never be too sure," he warned.

I would have argued the point normally but seeing as he had just arrested someone for murder, I didn't think it would be a convincing protest. We headed down Main St. toward my house and didn't say much.

"Listen, I know you probably feel you helped during the investigation, and you did. But you can't involve yourself in police business like that. It's not a game and you could have been hurt. You need to leave this kind of work to the professionals. I'm not saying there will be a next time, but next time, just come to us with what you have," Nick warned. I could tell he was trying not to offend me but that didn't mean it was working.

"And you would have listened to my ramblings? I mean, you would have followed up on it?" I responded in disbelief. He just gave me a look and I choose to interpret it as "of course" as opposed to "butt out." We kept walking in silence, and I wasn't really sure what to say after that.

"You got lucky. Either Roger or Lucy could have been dangerous. You don't have the training to deal with those situations," he finished. I didn't want to point out that when I was going into "those situations" I made a point of bringing someone who was trained … him. I don't know if he noticed my eye roll but if he did, he wisely chose to ignore it.

"So, I thought you and Tommy dated in high school?" Nick started. Wow … didn't see that one coming. Talk about a hard left at Albuquerque.

"Um … well, that's kind of a long story," I said. He just raised the eyebrow again. The whole not saying anything really does force someone to answer so I caved. "We sort of did. Tommy came out to Jess and I the summer before our junior year and asked us not to say anything. Senior year he was getting pressured from 'the guys' to date and I was trying to make sure my grades were good enough to pick my school, so it seemed like a good way to avoid peer pressure and not have to deal with actual relationship pressure." When we were seventeen, it made sense.

"You knew and just decided to give up your social life?" he pushed.

"First, you make it sound like I had one. If you will remember, I was painfully shy back then. And second, I didn't like what living a secret was doing to my friend. If all it took for me to make it easier for him was to pretend to be his girlfriend then sign me up," I answered. I had almost forgot that we had "dated." We were both in an awkward position back then and it made life easier. It didn't really occur to me that people would wonder about us after.

"Well, you had me fooled," Nick admitted. "What about now?"

"Now?" I have to admit I didn't know what he was talking about. "Now, Tommy and Mateo are happily engaged, and I'm divorced, run a successful business, have great kids, and a full life." I think that covered all the bases. Unless he was asking more about Tommy, and I wasn't sure what to do with that if he was.

"But are you seeing anyone?" Nick clarified.

"Oh, no. I have to admit it didn't really occur to me to have that kind of social life. I'm a bit obtuse when it comes to guys as Jess will tell you."

"Well, would you be opposed to seeing anyone?" Nick kept going.

"Umm … no. I guess not. I can't say anyone has asked lately," I added. I also hadn't been looking. I really did not do dating well. Hell, I even just sort of fell into a relationship with Mitch, but that story was for another day.

We had made it to my house and were walking up to the front porch. I took my keys out of my purse and Nick took them. He went in, did a brief safety check and handed me back my keys as I walked him to the door.

"Well, just so you know. I'll be asking, so be prepared to say yes." Nick put his hand on my cheek and kissed my forehead. "Good night, Maddy Carson."

"Good night," I whispered as I closed the door. Well, I certainly didn't see that coming.

Playlist:

Everything – Michael Buble
My Way – Frank Sinatra
I Will Survive – Gloria Gaynor – 70s version
Cats In the Cradle – Harry Chapin
That's What Friends Are For – Dionne Warwick and friends
Girls Just Want to Have Fun – Cyndi Lauper
Already Gone – Kelly Clarkson
Fancy – Reba McEntire
Daybreak – Barry Manilow
These Boots Are Made for Walking – Nancy Sinatra
Crush on You – The Jets

About the Author

Nancy Monroe is the pen name of a New Jersey attorney. When not plotting the death of random strangers she spends her time becoming obsessed with hobbies and then dropping then abandoning them for the next shiny object. She is the mother of two sons who are her pride and joy.

Nancy Monroe

Nancy Monroe